STAMPEDE!

Before Carole could finish speaking, Amelia turned on her heel, grabbed the bucket, and threw it against the pasture's metal watering trough. *Wham!* The crash was deafening. The Pony Clubbers jumped.

"Aiyh!" shouted a startled Carole. Patch leaped sideways so fast that the lead rope tore from Carole's hands. He squealed and reared; the other horses, also unnerved by the noise, milled in panic. Patch took off galloping for the safety of the field's far side. The other horses began to run, too. Suddenly it was a stampede.

Max was halfway across the field, in the center of the pasture, right in the path of the panicked horses.

"Max!" Carole cried. Max turned just as the first horses were upon him. Carole covered her eyes.

Max was going to be trampled!

THE SADDLE CLUB

HOBBYHORSE

BONNIE BRYANT

A SKYLARK BOOK

NEW YORK · TORONTO · LONDON · SYDNEY · AUCKLAND

RL 5, 009–012

HOBBYHORSE

A Bantam Skylark Book/November 1996

I would like to express my special thanks to Kimberly Brubaker Bradley for her help in the writing of this book.

1

LISA ATWOOD LOOKED out the window of her father's car. Across the highway, the Washington Monument went by in a flash. A line of tourists circled its base like a parade of ants, and Lisa wondered what it would be like to visit Washington, D.C., the way tourists did. Lisa lived in Willow Creek, Virginia, a small town just outside of D.C., and she'd spent a lot of time in the capital. Her mother had dragged her through every museum there.

Lisa leaned back and smiled. She didn't spend much time in museums these days. She didn't miss them.

Lisa's mother looked over the back of the seat. "We're almost at the airport, honey."

"I know, Mom." Lisa sat up a little straighter. It was a late Friday afternoon. Lisa and her parents were on their way to pick up Lisa's cousin, Amelia, who lived in New Jersey but was going to stay with them for a week while her parents went on vacation without her. It happened to be Lisa's winter break, but it wasn't Amelia's. She was being allowed to skip school.

"I bet you'll really enjoy Amelia, honey," Lisa's mother said. "I remember her as such a sweet child."

Lisa was not so sure. In the first place, her cousin was only nine years old. Lisa liked kids that age fine—in fact, she really enjoyed May, Jasmine, and Corey, three younger girls in Horse Wise, the Pony Club that Lisa and her friends belonged to.

Pony Clubs were sort of like Scout troops, except that they were all about horses. Long ago Lisa and her two best friends, Stevie and Carole, had also formed their own club called The Saddle Club. They'd recently discovered that May, Jasmine, and Corey had formed a similar club called Pony Tails. The younger girls seemed to look up to The Saddle Club, and Lisa liked that. She always tried to be nice to them.

There were other kids Amelia's age in Horse Wise, too, and most of them took lessons at Pine Hollow Stables, where Horse Wise met and where Lisa and her friends rode. The little kids were all nice as far as Lisa knew, but she wasn't interested in playing with them or spending a lot of time with them. She was too old, and she liked to spend time with her own friends.

Furthermore, Lisa didn't remember Amelia as a sweet child at all. In fact, the last time she'd seen her, three years earlier, she'd really disliked Amelia. Amelia had pulled Lisa's dog Dolly's tail and ripped up three of her favorite books. Amelia was a brat.

"It's lucky Amelia started riding this year, isn't it?" Lisa's father said. "You two will have a lot in common."

"I'm sure we will," Lisa said, with as much enthusiasm as she could muster. It wasn't a lot. Lisa was thankful that her cousin liked horses. She planned to take her cousin to Pine Hollow every day. Lisa would rather not have spent her week looking after Amelia, but at least she would be around horses. And she wouldn't have to take care of Amelia herself the whole time. Because of the school break, Max, the owner of Pine Hollow, was offering a special sort of mini riding camp just for the younger riders. Lisa knew it was sort of like day care, for kids too young to ride on their own or take care of themselves while their parents worked.

Lisa's father pulled the car into the airport parking garage. "We're right on time," Mrs. Atwood said, checking her watch. "I'm glad. I wouldn't want her to have to wait for us, the poor child. Lisa, don't you remember her last visit? She had the nicest manners of any child I've ever seen."

3

"Um-hm," Lisa murmured. So Amelia had known how to say please and thank you—so what? She'd thanked Lisa for letting her look at her books, and then she'd pulled the pages out! Lisa wondered if Amelia had asked Dolly's permission before pulling her tail.

"I was just so glad when my sister had Amelia," Lisa's mother continued. "They waited so long for that child."

Her friend Carole, Lisa reflected, was also an only child. But it hadn't seemed to turn Carole into a spoiled brat. In fact, Lisa didn't know a more caring person than Carole.

As soon as she thought of Carole, Lisa started to worry. When the car was parked, she got out and followed her parents into the airport, but as she walked all she could think of was Carole.

Unlike Lisa, Stevie and Carole each had her own horse. Stevie's mare, Belle, was a beautiful half-Arab, half-Saddlebred with a feisty personality that matched Stevie's. Carole's bay gelding, Starlight, had much of Carole's sweetness and talent. He was still young, but he was going to be a wonderful jumper, just as Lisa was sure Carole was going to be a famous rider someday—unless she decided to be a horse trainer, breeder, veterinarian, or one of the other horse professionals she was interested in becoming.

Carole was devoted to Starlight, and the horse received the best of care. But for the past few days, he had been

4

slightly lame in one of his front legs. Carole hadn't been able to ride him, and she'd been beside herself with worry. Lisa knew that if Starlight wasn't better by the time Carole got to the stable today, Carole was going to call Judy Barker, the vet. Lisa wished she could be there to support her friend.

Oh well, at least she's got Stevie, Lisa thought. When they had formed The Saddle Club, the three girls had vowed that they would always be ready to help each other out. That and being horse-crazy were the club's only rules.

Of course, Starlight's injury probably wasn't serious at all. Just like people, horses got minor aches and bruises all the time. Romeo, Polly Giacomin's horse, had strained his shoulder muscle a few weeks ago. Polly couldn't ride him for a few days, but Romeo had healed fine on his own. Lisa was sure Starlight's lameness was nothing serious, but since none of them knew what was causing it, they all worried a little. Carole, Lisa reflected, worried a *lot.*

Thinking about Carole's problem reminded Lisa of something else, and she started to laugh. She put her hand over her mouth when she realized that people in the airport were starting to stare at her. But it had been funny! Stevie loved practical jokes. In an effort to cheer Carole up, she'd put a small road apple—a round piece of horse manure—inside a boot belonging to Veronica diAngelo, the richest, snobbiest, most annoying rider at the stable. Veronica's shriek of horror as she put her foot into her boot had made all of them, including Carole, laugh until tears ran down their faces. The only person besides Veronica who hadn't seemed amused was Max.

Lisa jerked her thoughts back to the present. They had arrived at Amelia's gate, and the little girl was waiting for them, clinging to the hand of a rather harassed-looking flight attendant.

"Oh, I'm so glad to see you!" the flight attendant said with what sounded to Lisa like utter relief. Lisa wondered what the flight had been like. Had Amelia destroyed all the magazines on the plane?

"Auntie Eleanor! Uncle Richard!" Amelia gave a little cry of joy and wrapped herself around Mrs. Atwood's legs. "I'm so glad to see you! I thought you wouldn't come!"

Mrs. Atwood bent down and gave Amelia a hug.

The little girl had long brown hair cascading down the middle of her back and dark-brown heavily lashed eyes. She was perfectly attired in a plaid dress, tights, and little patent leather shoes. She had a navy blue wool coat over her arm and a matching wool hat on her head. She looked, in fact, a little young for her age, and Lisa wondered how she kept her clothes so neat.

"Here's your cousin Lisa," Mrs. Atwood said, peeling herself away from Amelia's tight embrace.

Amelia smiled shyly. "I'm so glad to meet you again,

6

Lisa," she said. "I just know we're going to have so much fun at your stable."

"I hope so," Lisa replied. She couldn't quite keep herself from sounding skeptical.

AMELIA WAS LIKE no other nine-year-old Lisa had ever met. Her manners were perfect, but somehow Lisa didn't trust them. While they waited for Amelia's suitcase, Lisa told her that they'd planned to stop for dinner on the way home, at The Spaghetti House, one of Lisa's favorite restaurants.

"Oh," Amelia said. "Oh, I'm sure that will be nice." But the pause between the first and second *oh* was a long one, and Amelia didn't quite look as though she thought it would be nice.

"Don't you like spaghetti, dear?" Mrs. Atwood asked.

"Oh, well. I'm sure there will be something there I can eat." Amelia smiled cheerfully. "Something. I'm sure."

"Well, we don't have to get spaghetti if you don't like it," Mr. Atwood said. "What do you like?"

Give me a break, Lisa thought. She had never known a nine-year-old who didn't like spaghetti.

"Well . . . I like pizza. That's sort of like spaghetti, isn't it?"

"Yes, it is," Mr. Atwood said heartily. "We'll stop for pizza, then."

Lisa had really wanted to go to The Spaghetti House. At

least I like pizza, she thought. She was glad Amelia hadn't expressed a desire for sushi. They'd all be settling down to plates of raw fish.

AT THE PIZZA PALACE the same sort of thing happened.

"Let's get pepperoni," Lisa suggested. She knew her mother didn't really like any other pizza toppings.

"Oh," Amelia said quietly. "Oh, okay."

"Don't you like pepperoni?" Mr. Atwood asked.

"I like sausage," Amelia said.

"Sausage it is!"

"But Dad!" Lisa protested. "You don't like sausage! Neither does Mom!"

"Oh, get pepperoni then," Amelia said hurriedly. "I'm sorry."

"No, that's okay, we all like sausage," Mr. Atwood assured her, giving Lisa a look that meant guests came first. They ended up with a large sausage pizza, with not a single slice of pepperoni in sight.

"I'm really looking forward to this riding camp," Amelia said as she sank her teeth into her first piece of pizza. "My mom has told me all about Pine Hollow. I'm sure it's almost as nice as the stable where I take lessons."

Lisa thought Pine Hollow was one of the nicest stables on earth. It might not be the fanciest, but it was nice in every sense of the word. She was just about to say so when her

8

mother said, "You really seem horse-crazy, Amelia. Just like Lisa."

Amelia glowed. "More than anything else in the world," she said. "I love horses."

Lisa smiled. "Me too."

"Windswept, the stable where I ride, is just filled with the most elegant people," Amelia continued. "My mother says you would be amazed, Aunt Eleanor."

Lisa couldn't believe what Amelia had just said. As if elegant people were important! Sometimes Lisa's mother got a little hung up on being a member of high society, and Lisa remembered that her aunt Marianne, Amelia's mother, could be the same way. It seemed as if Amelia was following right along.

"What about the horses?" Lisa asked.

"Oh, the horses!" Amelia's eyes widened. She grabbed the piece of pizza Lisa wanted next and stuffed it into her mouth before saying another word. Lisa thought Amelia's table manners, at least, could stand improvement.

Amelia dabbed at her mouth with her napkin. "I ride absolutely the best horse in the barn," she said, speaking to her aunt and uncle. "Her name is Star. She's a beautiful golden chestnut with the sweetest eyes, and she is so gentle."

This sounded pretty good to Lisa. But Amelia continued: "Her conformation is absolutely perfect. My trainer says there's not a better-looking or better-bred horse in the barn. Of course, she's rather high-spirited, and she can be quite difficult to handle, but I manage her just fine."

"Goodness! A little thing like you!" Mr. Atwood shot an amused look at his wife.

"My instructor, Ruth, says I'm a natural rider," Amelia said simply.

Lisa struggled to keep silent. She knew without a doubt that Star was neither high-spirited nor difficult to handle. Even if Amelia were the most natural rider in the world, she hadn't been riding long enough to deal with a difficult horse. Riding was hard, and good riding took time. Lisa also doubted Star had perfect conformation or breeding. Just like people, horses couldn't all be supermodel beautiful or tremendously athletic. Of course, some horses did have both incredible breeding and wonderful, gentle dispositions, but those horses were so valuable that they were almost never owned by stables that gave lessons. They were owned by very rich people.

Amelia was bragging. Didn't her parents notice? Lisa gritted her teeth. If she had bragged about being called a natural rider—which Max had once said she was—her parents would have told her to stop it.

Amelia prattled on about Star. She was the best horse, with the best personality, and everyone wanted to ride her all the time, but Amelia was the chosen one. Lisa began to realize that some smart instructor had convinced Amelia that Star was an advanced horse, rather than the beginner mount she had to be.

"My mother bought me a new pair of jodhpurs specially for the trip," Amelia said. "They're Pritchards. They cost over a hundred dollars. I have two pairs of them now."

"How lovely, dear," Mrs. Atwood said. Lisa pressed her lips together.

"Yes, and I'm probably going to get my own saddle soon, and Mummy said I might get a horse for my birthday. I probably will. I don't know if Ruth will sell Star, of course, because she is such a good horse, but if not we'll have to find one just like her."

Lisa couldn't believe this brat was getting her own horse. She hoped it wasn't true. It sounded as if Amelia was just getting carried away, but who knew for sure? Meanwhile, Lisa's parents seemed charmed by their niece's conversation.

When they finally got home, it was too late for Lisa to call Carole or Stevie, but the message light on the answering machine was blinking. Lisa hurried to play back the tape. It was Carole.

"Lisa"—Carole's voice quavered, as though she were near tears—"I called Judy, but she had to do an emergency colic surgery, and she couldn't see Starlight today. But I looked his symptoms up in a book—I'm so worried—call me when you can."

11

That was all. Lisa reset the tape. Whatever Starlight's problem was, it had to be awful for Carole to sound so upset. Lisa bit her lip. She'd have to wait until morning to find out what was wrong.

"Who was that?" Amelia demanded, walking up to Lisa. "What was she talking about? Does she have a horse?"

"That was my friend Carole." Lisa began to explain about Starlight.

"Why is her horse sick?" Amelia said. "What's wrong with it?"

Lisa closed her mouth and shut her eyes and silently counted to ten. If she didn't, she was going to say something rude.

"Star is *never* sick," Amelia said. "What were the other messages?"

"That's none of your business. It's my family's answering machine," Lisa said. "Besides, there weren't any other messages."

Amelia looked stricken. "Didn't my parents call?" she whispered.

Lisa hadn't even thought about that. She shook her head. "Sorry."

Amelia nodded and suddenly looked brighter. "I bet they called but just didn't want to leave a message. They'll call back soon."

Lisa's parents came in from the garage with Amelia's suit-

12

case. "Are you showing Amelia around, dear?" Mrs. Atwood asked.

"Uh, sure," Lisa said. "Amelia, this is the living room."

Amelia looked around. "Oh!" She gave a cry of delight. "Where did you get that hobbyhorse?"

Despite her bad mood, Lisa smiled. Amelia had discovered the most interesting object in the room. Between the two windows on the far side stood a beautiful antique hobbyhorse that Lisa's parents had bought in England. It was made of polished wood with a real horsehair mane and tail and a real leather saddle and bridle, and it was more than two hundred years old. Lisa loved it.

Amelia rushed forward and hugged the little horse. "Oh, it's beautiful! Look at its saddle! Can I ride it?"

"No," Lisa said quickly. Amelia froze.

"It's just for decoration," Mrs. Atwood explained. "It's very old and fragile."

"It was made for little kids, anyway," Lisa said. "You're too big."

Amelia frowned and didn't say anything. She smoothed the hobbyhorse's mane and arranged the reins so that they rested on the saddle. Lisa wondered what she was thinking. It was impossible to tell.

Lisa was relieved when her parents suggested that it might be time for Amelia to go to bed. Tomorrow would be a busy day, starting with the usual Saturday-morning Horse Wise meeting. Even though it was a little early for Lisa to go to bed, she followed her parents and Amelia up to the guest room.

Amelia didn't want to sleep in the guest room. She didn't want to be alone in a strange house. It was really scary. Before Lisa knew quite what had happened, Amelia was being tucked into Lisa's four-poster bed, and Lisa's mother was handing Lisa a sleeping bag so that she could sleep on the floor.

Lisa rolled herself into her bag and shut her eyes, but she couldn't sleep. She fretted over Starlight and Carole. She tried to block out the sound of Amelia's earth-shattering snores. She wished the floor weren't quite so hard.

It was going to be a very long week.

2

IN THE MORNING Lisa woke to find Amelia rummaging through the drawers of her desk. "What do you think you're doing?" Lisa demanded, sitting up and climbing out of her sleeping bag.

"Just looking," Amelia replied. "Who's John Brightstar?"

"Were you reading my letters?" Lisa asked in amazement. John was a friend of hers who lived on a ranch out West.

"No, I just looked at the envelopes," Amelia said. "He wrote his return address on them. Is he your boyfriend?"

He wasn't, but that was none of Amelia's business. "You're not allowed to look through my drawers," Lisa said. She took her letters away from Amelia and jammed them back into the drawer. "You're not allowed to look through any of my stuff."

"But I'm company," Amelia said with a puzzled frown. "I'm supposed to be able to do whatever I want."

"Not in my room," Lisa said. She grabbed her clothes and went to the bathroom to dress and brush her teeth. What a way to start the morning!

When she came back into her room, she found Amelia sitting on the bed, which she'd made neatly. Amelia had folded Lisa's sleeping bag, too, and put her own nightgown into her suitcase. She was completely dressed in a turtleneck, wool sweater, and her hundred-dollar jodhpurs, and she'd braided her hair nicely. But the thing Lisa noticed first was that Amelia was reading one of her best books!

"Give that back!" Lisa cried, snatching it out of Amelia's hands. It was an old copy of *Black Beauty*, with beautiful color illustrations, and Lisa loved it. She didn't want Amelia messing it up.

"I was just reading it," Amelia protested in a hurt voice. "I didn't know I wasn't allowed to look at your books."

Lisa realized that Amelia was probably old enough now to be trusted with her books. "I'm sorry," she said. "I guess you can look at them. Just be careful, okay?"

Amelia still looked hurt, but she smiled. "Okay. Can we go to the stable now?"

Lisa smiled back. At least there was one thing about

16

Amelia she could stand. It was awfully early, but Lisa knew
Carole would be there early today, and she hoped Stevie
would be, too. "Great idea," she said.

LISA'S MOTHER DROVE them to Pine Hollow. On the way Lisa
thought again about the Pony Tails and how glad she was
that they would be around this week. They might take
Amelia off her hands. "Do you have lots of friends at your
stable at home?" she asked the little girl.

Amelia looked out the car window for a long time without answering. "The other girls at my stable are not very
friendly," she finally said. She looked sideways at her aunt.
"They're elegant people, you understand, they just aren't
very friendly."

Lisa sighed. She could guess what that meant. Amelia had
probably acted bratty in front of the people at her stable and
no one there liked her. "The people at Pine Hollow are very
friendly," she assured her cousin. She knew it was true, but
would they be friendly toward Amelia? Lisa hoped so.

THE FIRST PERSON they saw when they went into the stable
was Max. Lisa introduced Amelia to him. Amelia shook his
hand gravely, a smile lighting her small face. "I'm very
pleased to meet you," she said. "Thank you for letting me
ride here while I'm visiting Lisa."

"You're welcome," Max said. He smiled at Amelia and

raised his eyebrows at Lisa as if to say he was impressed. Lisa wished she could explain that Amelia's manners were only skin deep.

"Look!" she said instead. "There's Stevie and Carole!" She grabbed Amelia's hand and pulled her down the aisle.

"Bye, Max!" Amelia said, waving, as Lisa dragged her away.

"Carole!" Lisa hugged her friend. "How is Starlight?"

Carole and Stevie were both standing beside Starlight in the center of the stable aisle. Stevie held Starlight's lead rope. Carole had filled a bucket with warm water and set it on the floor. She was about to coax Starlight to put his sore foot into it. "Good boy," she crooned to him. To Lisa she added, with a grimace, "He's the same as yesterday. Still lame. Judy's going to try to come out today, but she's still tied up with the colicking horse."

Lisa nodded. It was important that Starlight see a vet, but his lameness probably wasn't an emergency. "This is my cousin Amelia," she said. Carole and Stevie both said hi, but neither of them did more than glance at the girl. They were both focused on Starlight.

"Tell me what you were thinking, Carole," Lisa said, moving to Starlight's side. The gelding wore his usual calm, pleasant expression. He didn't seem to be feeling too awful.

"Well, it could be an abscess," Carole explained. "That's basically a pocket of infection in his hoof, and if that's true,

18

then he'll be okay as soon as we take care of it." She stroked Starlight's neck as she talked. She knew he didn't look too bad, but when he walked he limped, and his head bobbed in pain every time he put weight on his sore foot. Carole could barely stand to see him in pain. He'd never had anything seriously wrong before.

"Abscesses are pretty common," Stevie said.

"Didn't Patch have one last year?" Lisa asked.

Stevie nodded.

"As long as it *is* an abscess," Carole said. "Look at the way he's pointing with his foot." Lisa and Stevie looked. Starlight was standing with his right front foot—his sore one—out in front of him.

"He's trying to take his weight off it," Lisa guessed. "Because it hurts him."

Carole nodded miserably. "I was reading in my horse books last night. It's a classic sign of navicular disease."

"Oh no," Stevie said.

"What's that?" Amelia asked. She reached up to pat Starlight's nose as she spoke. "Did he do something wrong?"

"Of course not," Carole said sharply. "It isn't his fault." As Carole bent to put Starlight's hoof into the bucket of water, Lisa could see that she was scowling.

Amelia nodded. "I guess not, because he looks like a nice horse. He's really beautiful."

"Thank you," Carole said, straightening up. She bit her

19

lip. She'd been struggling all morning not to cry. The navicular bones were some of the tiny ones in a horse's foot. They corresponded roughly to the human wrist.

"It's too bad he's hurt," Amelia continued. "I'd really like to ride him."

Carole grinned at the little girl, but then she realized that Amelia was serious. "You couldn't ride Starlight," she said. "He's not used in lessons." Carole knew Lisa's cousin was a beginning rider, and beginning riders had no business on spirited horses like Starlight.

"Carole is the only person who rides Starlight," Lisa explained patiently. "He's still young, and she's training him."

Amelia drew her mouth into a pout. "But I want to ride him," she said, as if that were the only important thing.

Stevie and Lisa exchanged looks. "But he's hurt," Lisa said.

"I understand." Amelia nodded. "What are you soaking his foot in?"

"Water mixed with some salts Max gave me," Carole explained. She went on to describe exactly what sort of salts they were, how much she put in the bucket, and how often and for how long she used them.

Lisa and Stevie smiled at each other. It was entirely like Carole to recite all the tiny details of her horse's care. Most little kids, even ones who liked horses, would have been bored, but Amelia listened carefully, nodding and peering into the bucket. When Starlight started to lift his foot out of the bucket, Amelia said "Whoa" and gently pushed it back in, even before Carole could.

"She really likes horses," Stevie whispered to Lisa in a tone of approval. "I don't know, Lisa, she doesn't seem that bad. After everything you told us about her, I expected a real brat."

Lisa rolled her eyes. "Sometimes she's not that bad, but just give her time and you'll see what I mean," she said.

"Hey, Carole," Stevie said more loudly, "tell Lisa your good news."

Carole looked at Starlight and frowned. "What good n— oh, right! Lisa, Max asked me to be an assistant instructor for the kids' camp this week. He said that since I couldn't ride Starlight, I could help him. I'll still be doing something around horses."

"That sounds great!" Lisa was happy for her friend. Being an assistant instructor would be fun, and Carole would learn a lot. But when she looked at Carole, Lisa could see that her friend wasn't really thinking about her good news. She was worrying about her horse.

"HELLO, MAX!" LISA heard May Grover shout outside the stable. Lisa stood on tiptoes to look out a window.

"Hey, it's the Pony Tails! Amelia, come on, I want you to meet them. Carole, we'll be right back."

21

Corey, Jasmine, and May all had ponies of their own that they kept in their backyards. May's father had a four-horse trailer, and he often brought May's pony, Macaroni, Corey's pony, Samurai, and Jasmine's pony, Outlaw, over to Pine Hollow for Horse Wise, riding lessons, and other activities. Since the little girls would be going to the school-break camp, they'd arranged to have their ponies spend the whole week at Pine Hollow. That way Mr. Grover wouldn't have to keep bringing them back and forth. Max had three empty stalls he was letting them use, but before Mr. Grover arrived with the ponies, the girls had to get the stalls ready.

Lisa pulled Amelia down the aisle just as all three Pony Tails disappeared into the feed room. They emerged with wheelbarrows and pitchforks and hurried to the empty stalls. Lisa hurried after them. "Hey, guys! This is my cousin Amelia. She's going to spend the week here and ride in the camp."

May stopped shoveling sawdust into her wheelbarrow just long enough to smile. "Super!" she said. "We're going to have a lot of fun!" She wheeled the barrow across the aisle and dumped it into an empty stall.

"Hi, Amelia!" Corey said. "I'm Corey. Lisa told us you were coming." She hung Samurai's special water bucket in his stall. Samurai could be particular, and he only liked to drink out of one special bucket.

22

"You can help us if you want to," Jasmine added. "Grab a pitchfork."

"Why would I want to do that?" Amelia asked. She sounded genuinely confused.

All the Pony Tails seemed surprised by her reaction. "Because it's fun," Jasmine answered.

Amelia shrugged in a way that reminded Lisa instantly of Veronica diAngelo, her least favorite person. Lisa sighed. How could Amelia be so interested in Starlight's treatment and so uninterested in preparing some stalls? To Lisa, they were both part of the same thing: taking care of horses.

"At my stable," Amelia said, "we don't *work*."

Aha, Lisa thought. *The snob factor difference.*

Corey and May stopped working and stared at Amelia. "At our stable," Jasmine said, "we do."

Amelia blushed, then swept a glance over them. Her gaze rested longest, and most pointedly, at the ragged hole worn through the knee of May's jodhpurs. "Of course," she said with a shrug, "maybe you need to work. I don't. At Windswept, the stable where I ride, everything is the very best. The best sort of people ride there."

Lisa winced. Amelia was switching into full brat mode. So much for Lisa's hope that Amelia could spend the week with the Pony Tails. She could already guess that they weren't going to like Amelia any better than Lisa did.

"You should see the horse I ride," Amelia continued. "Her name is Star, and she's exceptionally well bred. She's the nicest horse at Windswept. Of course she isn't easy to ride, but my instructor says I'm naturally talented, and I handle her just fine. I'm a very advanced rider for my age."

May looked directly at Lisa. "Is that true?" she asked.

Lisa wanted to say "Of course not, she's being a horrible bragging brat"—but then she'd never seen Amelia ride. "I don't know," she said after a pause. "I don't think so."

Amelia flushed red. She looked furious. "Lisa! I told you all about it!"

"I know you did," Lisa said uncomfortably.

"How long have you been riding?" May cut in.

Amelia lifted her head proudly. "Since last September."

"Ohhh," May said softly. She and her friends went back to their work.

May had been riding since she was three years old, and Jasmine and Corey had both ridden for a long time, too. Amelia might think that four months was a long time to be riding, but the Pony Tails weren't going to agree. Even a naturally talented rider needed longer than four months to become a good rider.

"Come on," Lisa said, reaching to touch Amelia's shoulder. "Let's go meet some more horses. I haven't introduced you to Prancer."

Amelia swerved away from Lisa's touch. "I *told* Lisa," she

said to the Pony Tails, in a loud voice. "She just must not have been listening. Star is a very good horse, she's very beautiful, she's very hard to ride—"

"Excuse me," May cut in, "but I think my dad just pulled up. We have to go get our ponies out of the horse trailer now." The Pony Tails hardly looked at Amelia as they left the stable.

Amelia stared after them openmouthed. "Do they all have their own ponies?" she asked in a whisper.

"Yeah," Lisa said. "They do." She felt bad. On the one hand, Amelia had gotten what she deserved; but on the other hand, Lisa felt as if she should have stuck up for her cousin. Lisa was beginning to understand that bragging was Amelia's way of trying to be liked. It wasn't a good way, but maybe she just didn't know any better.

Amelia stamped her foot. "I don't like the people at this stable, either!" she said.

Lisa sighed. Feeling sorry for Amelia seemed like a waste of time.

LISA LED AMELIA back to the other end of the stable and stopped outside Belle's stall. Stevie was inside, grooming her beautiful mare. "This is Stevie's horse, Belle," Lisa said to Amelia. "And next to her is the horse I usually ride, Prancer."

"Oh, Stevie! She's beautiful!" Amelia clasped her hands and looked up at Belle with rapt adoration. Lisa stifled a giggle. Belle was beautiful. She was a bright bay with a shiny black mane and tail and white markings on her face and forehead that looked like an upside-down exclamation point. Still, it seemed to Lisa that Amelia was overdoing it. Belle wasn't *that* beautiful.

"And Prancer! Lisa, you didn't tell me she was *this* gorgeous!" Amelia held her hands flat under Prancer's nose, and as the mare sniffed them, her ears pricked forward with interest. Prancer always seemed to love children. "She's almost as pretty as Star," Amelia said. Lisa glowed with pride until she saw Stevie grinning at her. Then she realized that Amelia was complimenting Prancer just as extravagantly as she had complimented Belle—in other words, overextravagantly.

"I can see you're a fine judge of horses," Carole commented dryly. She'd overheard the whole exchange. Lisa and Stevie laughed a little self-consciously.

"I'm glad you like them," Lisa told Amelia. "They're both good horses."

Amelia looked from Prancer to Belle and back. "I just don't know how I'll ever pick between them," she said. "I want to ride them both!"

Carole recalled how Amelia had wanted to ride Starlight, too. Even though the younger girl was interested in horses, she clearly hadn't learned a lot about them yet. She still didn't realize that riding an advanced horse was dangerous for a beginner. Amelia certainly couldn't ride Prancer; what's more, she wouldn't enjoy herself if she tried. Most likely she would end up scaring herself and confusing Prancer.

"Well, you can't ride Belle," Stevie said quickly, before

Carole could speak. "She's my horse, and no one else rides her. I'm training her. Max will tell you which horse you'll ride."

Amelia turned her head away. "Fine," she said sulkily. "If Belle doesn't know what she's doing, I'd rather not ride her anyway. I'll ride Prancer. That'll be okay, won't it, Lisa? It's not like she's your horse."

"No!" Lisa said, a little stung. "It won't be okay! I'm riding Prancer this week, and anyway, she's never used for beginners. She used to be a racehorse, and she's still hot-headed sometimes."

Amelia stamped her foot. Carole and Stevie stared at her. Lisa thought that the foot-stamping was getting annoying. "I'm not a beginner!" Amelia said. "Star is a very difficult horse!"

Lisa lost her patience. "Enough about Star!" she said. "You'll ride whatever horse Max gives you, and it won't be Prancer because I'm riding her!" It was bad enough that Lisa had to share her bedroom and her privacy and her week with Amelia. She was not sharing Prancer, not even on the trillion-to-one chance that Max would actually allow it. "And quit stamping," she said to her cousin. "You look like a three-year-old."

Amelia crossed her arms and stamped her foot as hard as she could. "You're mean!" she yelled at Lisa. "You just want to keep all the good horses to yourself!"

28

Lisa didn't know what to do, but yelling back at Amelia was only going to make the situation worse.

Stevie fought a strong urge to laugh. Amelia's face was crimson with anger, and she looked about as sweet as a cobra ready to strike. Stevie's three brothers sometimes seemed like incredible brats, but they could take lessons from Amelia.

Carole was momentarily relieved that she was an only child. She caught Lisa's eye and shook her head slightly. Lisa nodded back. They both knew that the argument couldn't be allowed to continue. Max would not approve.

"What's going on?" said a familiar, infuriatingly cool voice. "Is there a little problem here? I hope you all aren't scaring Danny."

Amelia turned, her tantrum suspended.

"Amelia," Lisa said, "meet Veronica diAngelo. She's in Horse Wise, and that's her horse, Danny, in the stall on the end. Veronica, this is my cousin Amelia. She's here for the week."

Veronica looked the younger girl up and down. "Well, Amelia," she said, "it's nice to meet you. Lisa got our introductions backward, you know. You should have been introduced to me. But I won't hold it against her. She's still learning her manners, isn't she?"

Stevie and Carole stared as if Veronica were speaking Chinese. Lisa understood and sighed. Her mother had drilled her on the art of the social introduction—the less important person was always introduced to the more important person. It was the sort of social rule that Lisa found utterly trivial—and she wasn't sure she'd call Veronica Amelia's social superior, anyway. Amelia was a brat, but Veronica was in a brat class by herself.

Amelia stared at Veronica's elegant clothes and perfectly styled hair. "You're wearing Pritchard breeches," she said.

"Of course," said Veronica. "They're the best."

"I've got Pritchard jods on," Amelia said confidingly.

"Do you really?" Veronica checked the label. "You do! Fantastic. You're a much better dresser than your cousin, aren't you?"

Amelia beamed. "Look, Amelia—" Lisa began, in a much calmer voice, now that she'd had time to regain her composure.

"*Horse Wise!*" Max called down the aisle. "Come to order!" Stevie hurried to take Belle's halter off.

Veronica put her arm around Amelia's shoulder. "Come on," she said. "I'll introduce you to my particular friends. I'm sure Lisa hasn't bothered."

Veronica's "particular friends" were a group of snobby girls who hung on Veronica's every word. "The only people I've met are the Pony Tails," Amelia said, as she started down the aisle with Veronica. "They seemed okay."

30

"Oh, *well*, you don't need to hang around them," Veronica assured her. "They're not society."

Amelia nodded. "May had a hole in her jodhpurs."

THE SADDLE CLUB watched all this with disbelieving eyes. "I take back what I said before," Stevie commented. "Lisa, she's worse than you said!"

"She might not be that bad," Carole said. She slipped her arm through Lisa's. "But if she is, you can count on our help."

"Yeah," Stevie said. "We'll hog-tie her and leave her in the loft all week. Lisa, whatever you do, get her away from Veronica. It's scary, how well they get along."

As they were going into the office, Lisa pulled May to one side. "I've got a favor to ask you," she said. "A big one."

May looked at the ground. "Uh-huh," she said without enthusiasm.

"I know it's going to take some effort, but would you please try to be nice to Amelia?"

May looked up at Lisa and shifted her weight from foot to foot. "She seems like kind of a snob," she whispered.

"I know she seems that way," Lisa replied. "I think she might not be very good at making friends. You don't have to do stuff with her. Just try to be nice to her, because she's going to be riding with you and everything. You and Jasmine and Corey—please?" May looked doubtful. "As a special favor to The Saddle Club?" Lisa asked.

"Okay," May said at last. "I'll try."

"Thank you!" Lisa felt relieved. Now she didn't have to feel so guilty about not sticking up for Amelia before, and if she was lucky, Amelia would still spend some time hanging around the Pony Tails. Lisa did not want to spend every minute of the next week with her cousin. She didn't really want to spend any minutes with her, period.

Inside the office, the riders crowded together, most of them sitting on the floor. They were all talking and laughing while they waited for Max to come in and start the meeting. At the front of the room they'd left a space for Max to stand, next to a big chalkboard used during lectures and demonstrations. Lisa joined Carole and Stevie toward the back, near the windows. May squirmed her way to the first row of kids, where she sat between Corey and the wall. Amelia, Lisa noticed, was sitting by herself on the side of the room. Veronica was only a few feet away, talking animatedly with Betsy Cavanaugh. She seemed to have forgotten Amelia already.

"Carole and I tried to sit next to her," Stevie whispered to Lisa. "As soon as we sat down, she moved."

Lisa looked at Amelia's pinched, stubborn expression and sighed. She watched May settle herself between her friends.

She went up to her cousin and knelt down. "Why don't you come sit with us?" she asked.

Amelia shrugged. "Your friends aren't very nice. Stevie laughed when I said I wanted to ride Prancer."

"I don't think Stevie meant to laugh. Give them another chance."

"I don't want to. I like sitting here by Veronica."

"Why don't you go sit by the Pony Tails? They're really nice, once you get to know them."

"Oh, them." Amelia raised her voice so that the entire room could hear. "May's parents must not know much about horses if they let her run around in awful clothes like that."

The entire room went suddenly silent. All of Horse Wise had heard Amelia's ridiculous pronouncement. Lisa blushed with shame.

"Oh boy," Stevie said to Carole, under her breath. "I bet May slugs Amelia for that."

Nearly everyone liked May, but she was not known for keeping her temper. Everyone in the room seemed to be holding their breath, waiting for May to respond.

For a moment, May looked stunned. Then she looked furious. She opened her mouth, then looked at Lisa, Carole, and Stevie, swallowed hard, and shut it. She turned slightly so that she was no longer facing Amelia and kept her eyes on the front of the room.

"Good for her!" Carole whispered.

Jasmine and Corey looked plenty angry, too. "You don't know anything!" Jasmine said to Amelia, in a voice of disbelief. "May's dad is a horse trainer!"

"So what?" Amelia asked rudely.

Jasmine's eyes grew wide. May reached out, still without looking at Amelia, and tapped Jasmine on the shoulder. Reluctantly Jasmine turned around, too.

Amelia's face was slightly pink, but she looked more triumphant than anything else, as if she had somehow won a victory against the other girls. She smiled at Veronica, who smiled back in a condescending way. Lisa was hot with shame.

Max came in and shut the door behind him. His pleasant greeting dispelled some of the tension that Amelia's rudeness had generated. All the kids turned their attention to Max, and Lisa felt herself relaxing a little.

"Before we begin, I want to introduce a visitor to all of you," Max started out. Lisa felt herself go tense again. "Lisa's cousin is here for the week," Max continued. "She'll be joining us in Horse Wise today and at camp all week. Lisa, care to introduce us?"

If Lisa had had a choice, she would never even have admitted that Amelia was her cousin. But she didn't have a choice. She stood up and grabbed Amelia by the arm.

Amelia stood, too, with a picture-perfect smile on her face. "This is Amelia," Lisa said, and sat back down.

Max looked surprised at her abruptness. "Uh . . . Amelia, maybe you'd like to tell us something about yourself."

The little girl beamed. "Well, I'm really glad I get to come to your camp. I'm still learning how to ride, but I love horses and love learning everything I can about them."

"Unbelievable," Lisa muttered.

Max smiled at Amelia. "We're very glad to have you here," he said. "Why don't you come up to the front, where you can see? Polly's going to be giving us a demonstration on bits. May, do you mind scooting over?"

May slid half an inch to the left, increasing the space between herself and the wall. Amelia cooed, "Oh, thank you, Max." She went to May's right, cramming herself between May and Corey. May and Corey had no choice but to give her room, but neither of them looked at her.

Carole shook her head in amazement. "It's like Dr. Jekyll and Mr. Hyde," she said softly to Stevie and Carole. At the front of the room, Polly was laying out various bits and bridles.

"Who're they?" Stevie asked.

Lisa frowned. "*He*, not *they*. It's a story about this guy

35

named Dr. Jekyll, who turns from a quiet gentleman into a mouth-foaming monster in two seconds flat."

"Just like Amelia," Lisa groaned.

Stevie giggled. "It's perfect. When Amelia comes around, all the other kids are going to Hyde."

"I made May promise to be nice to her," Lisa said, shaking her head. "I'm going to have to buy the Pony Tails ice cream cones by the time this week is through."

"Ice cream cones?" Stevie asked. "Maybe you haven't been paying attention. Between the way Amelia is acting and the way they're taking it, you're already up to hot fudge sundaes."

Lisa groaned and agreed. "By next Saturday, they may never have to pay for their own ice cream again."

4

"EVERYBODY THANK POLLY for that excellent presentation," Max said. The members of Horse Wise clapped enthusiastically. Carole hadn't thought Polly's presentation was all that good—she'd forgotten to mention rubber-mouth training bits, and she'd failed to explain completely the difference between D-ring and egg-butt snaffles—but she figured Polly had done her best, so she clapped hard anyway.

Lisa stole another glance at Amelia. The little girl had listened with intense interest to every word Polly had said. Lisa didn't understand her cousin at all.

"So now it's time to ride," Max continued. "Now, as you know, the school horses have had to stay in their stalls a lot lately because of the cold weather. Since it was so much warmer this morning, Red and I turned most of them out in the back pasture for some exercise. We'll have to go get them and groom them.

"Listen up," Max said, holding up his hand. "I want you to remember that horses sometimes behave differently when they're together in a herd. They follow different instincts. Sometimes even calm horses can act dangerously. So, while I want you all to get the halter and lead rope of the horse you'll be riding and go out to the pasture gate, I want only a few of you older kids in the pasture with me. We'll put the halters on the horses and lead them out the gate. Okay?"

Lisa nodded to herself. She'd been around herds of horses on her friend's ranch out West, and she knew what Max said made sense. In a herd, horses tried to dominate one another. They sometimes reared or kicked at each other. Humans had to be careful not to get in the way.

Carole raised her hand. "Max, our horses are already in. We can help you."

Max smiled. "Thank you. You three would be just right."

The riders all left the office. Stevie and Carole hesitated at the door, waiting for Lisa, who was waiting for Amelia. Amelia walked up to Max instead. Taking his hand confidingly, she asked, "Which horse should I ride today?"

Max smiled. "I'm going to give you a horse named Patch. You'll like him. He's a nice guy."

Lisa and Carole both nodded. Patch was old, gentle, and comfortable. He was the best choice for a young beginner, particularly one Max had never seen ride. Patch would take good care of Amelia.

Amelia pushed her lower lip out the slightest bit. "But I'd rather ride Prancer," she said. "Can I, please? I already met her, and I could tell she really loved me. Please, Max, please?"

Max bent down so that his face was even with Amelia's. He spoke very kindly. "I'm sure you liked Prancer. She's a pretty horse, and she really seems to love kids, I know. But sometimes she acts silly when she's being ridden. I don't think she's a good choice for you. Patch will be much better."

Amelia's beautiful eyes filled with tears. "Please?" she whispered.

Max gave Amelia a little squeeze on the chin.

"Oh, gross," Lisa whispered. "Can't he see what she's doing? She just wants to get her own way."

"You can't ride Prancer today," Max said. "You can ride Patch."

"What about tomorrow? Can I ride Prancer tomorrow? Please, Max!"

"You know," Max said, "I don't think you realize what a super horse Patch is. You're really going to like him."

"Does he jump?" Amelia asked.

39

Max nodded. "Yes, he does."

Stevie snickered, and Carole elbowed her. Lisa grinned. They knew they were all thinking the same thing. Patch would jump any fence willingly and safely, but not at all elegantly. "Jumps like an elephant would," Stevie muttered.

"Is he well bred?" Amelia asked.

Lisa sighed. She wished Amelia would get over her obsession with pedigrees and social standing. A horse's breeding was not nearly as important as its personality and talent.

Max paused. "Er . . . yes. Yes, he's very well bred."

Carole knew Max wasn't really lying—so long as he interpreted "well bred" to mean mannerly and kind. Patch was descended from a plow horse and a part draft horse, neither of them pedigreed.

"Okay," Amelia said reluctantly. "If Patch is really good, I'll ride him today. But I want to ride Prancer tomorrow."

"Come on, Amelia," Lisa said.

Max looked up at The Saddle Club. "Carole, why don't you take Amelia and show her where the halters are? After all, you are my assistant instructor."

Carole smiled. "Sure!" She took Amelia by the hand and led her down the stable aisle. As she went, Lisa and Stevie could hear her saying, "Now, there are a lot of important things to know about halters . . ."

"Phew!" Lisa said, when they were on their way out of the

40

stable. "Just getting to spend one moment away from Amelia makes me feel better!"

"What I'm glad about is that Carole's going to enjoy being an assistant instructor," Stevie said. "And it gives her something to think about besides Starlight's foot. When I got here this morning she was in his stall, crying. She tried to pretend that she wasn't when she saw me."

"She was crying?" Lisa asked. "I knew she was upset, but I guess I didn't know she was that upset. Do you know anything about navicular disease?"

"Not really," Stevie said. "We'll have to ask Carole about it."

"It must be pretty serious if she was crying. We'll talk to her as soon as we can," Lisa said, and they hurried on to the pasture.

CAROLE TOOK AMELIA into the tack room and showed her the row of halters hanging on the wall. "This one belongs to Patch," Carole said. She pulled it off the high hook, attached a lead rope to it, and handed it to Amelia. Amelia slung it expertly onto her shoulder. Carole smiled. Whatever her shortcomings might be, the girl really did seem to care about horses.

"Why do the hats spell *brat?*" Amelia asked. Carole groaned. A bunch of extra riding helmets hung on a pegboard on the tack room wall, and it was one of Stevie's

41

favorite pastimes to arrange them so they spelled a word. When had Stevie had time to make them say *brat*? Carole couldn't remember Stevie being out of her sight once all morning.

"Umm, I don't think they're meant to spell anything," Carole said. "I think they just accidentally got put up like that." She led Amelia out of the room. To get to the back pasture, they had to walk past the stalls with the Pony Tails' ponies. Corey, Jasmine, and May were all tacking up. As Carole and Amelia walked by, the Pony Tails burst into fits of laughter. Amelia was chattering about halters and didn't seem to notice, but Carole had to stifle a giggle. So that was who had rearranged the hats! The Pony Tails had found a way to get even without—quite—breaking their promise to Lisa.

OUTSIDE, MAX RATTLED a bucket of grain near the gate until the whole herd of horses stopped grazing and began to walk slowly toward him. "Okay," he said, consulting his list, "Stevie, you get Nickel and give him to Joey. Lisa, find Barq for Betsy. Hi, Carole!" Max looked up and grinned. "Since you're taking care of Amelia, you can get Patch."

Amelia waited at the gate while The Saddle Club slipped into the pasture. "I'm riding Patch," she announced importantly. "Max said he was a very good horse. One of the best."

42

Jessica Adler, who was Amelia's age and a friend of all the Pony Tails, spoke up. "He is a good horse, and he's a very, very, very easy horse. I rode Patch in my first lesson, but when I got to be a good rider Max let me have someone else."

Across the field, Stevie and Lisa watched the exchange.

"Look at Amelia. She's getting all red and mad again," Stevie said.

"I know," Lisa said with a shake of her head. There was nothing she could do about it. Both Barq and Nickel had decided that they liked their freedom, and while they weren't running from the girls, they had reversed direction and were walking to the far end of the field. Stevie and Lisa had to walk after them.

"Amelia," Carole called from the edge of the pasture, "come over here by the fence. There are some things I need to tell you."

Carole thought Amelia looked a little blotchy and grouchy again. She briefly wondered why, then quit worrying about it. Amelia's natural expression wasn't all that pleasant anyway. Probably nothing was wrong.

"See?" Carole said, "I've wrapped the lead rope around Patch's neck, so I can hang on to him while I put his halter on."

"That's Patch?" Amelia sounded disgusted.

Carole patted the horse affectionately. "Yeah, silly boy,

he found some mud to roll in. He probably had an itch on his back. It's going to take you a while to groom him."

"But he's ugly," Amelia said. "He doesn't look like Prancer at all. And Jessica said he was—"

Patch had big knees and a thick head and wasn't built very well, but he had a wonderful heart. "He's a good horse," Carole interrupted, speaking firmly. "Now, listen, Amelia, because this is important. The one thing you have to know about Patch is that loud noises frighten him. You have to be careful—"

Max had hung his metal grain bucket on the fence post near Amelia. Before Carole could finish speaking, Amelia turned on her heel, grabbed the bucket, and threw it against the pasture's metal watering trough. *Wham!* The crash was deafening. The Pony Clubbers jumped.

"Aiyh!" shouted a startled Carole. Patch leaped sideways so fast that the lead rope tore from Carole's hands. He squealed and reared; the other horses, also unnerved by the noise, milled in panic. Patch took off galloping for the safety of the field's far side. The other horses began to run, too. Suddenly it was a stampede.

Lisa couldn't believe her eyes. All the horses in the pasture were galloping out of control. She and Stevie ran for the pasture fence. Lisa looked back over her shoulder. "Oh no!" she screamed. "Max!"

Max had decided to come out and help Lisa and Stevie.

44

He was halfway across the field, in the center of the pasture, right in the path of the panicked horses.

"Max!" Carole's cry echoed Lisa's. Max turned just as the first horses were upon him. Carole covered her eyes.

Max was going to be trampled!

IT WAS TOO LATE for Max to try to escape. Carole uncovered her eyes and saw Max's own eyes widen, but he kept his body perfectly still. Carole knew that the horses wouldn't deliberately bump Max, but if one horse ran into another or didn't pay attention, Max could be trampled.

The horses swerved around him. One of them knocked Max's hat to the ground, but in a moment Max was safe. The horses galloped down to the far end of the field and whinnied and snorted and milled around. They were no longer running as a herd, and the danger was over.

Carole looked for Lisa and Stevie and was relieved to see

them on the outside of the fence. They slipped back through the rails and caught up to Max, and all three came back to the gate.

The Pony Clubbers stood in shocked silence. They all realized how close Max had come to disaster. The only person making any noise at all was Amelia, who was sobbing violently. Carole hoped that Amelia had learned her lesson. If Max had been killed, it would have been her fault.

"What happened?" Lisa asked as she came hurrying up. She bent over her cousin. "Amelia?"

"Max!" Amelia launched herself, still sobbing, at him. She threw her arms around his legs, and when he bent down she cried against his shoulder. "Oh, Max! I was so scared! I thought you were going to die!" She sobbed harder, and the Pony Clubbers clustered around her while Max patted her shoulder. Lisa felt sorry for Amelia. Whatever had spooked Patch had obviously spooked Amelia, too.

"Patch is a scary horse!" Amelia sobbed.

Lisa remembered the "scary" guest room. Her back was still aching slightly from sleeping on the floor. Her sympathy toward Amelia began to fade.

"It's okay," Max soothed her. "I'm okay, Patch is okay, you're okay. Nobody got hurt."

With all her crying, Amelia had claimed everyone's attention. Everyone looked concerned about her—everyone,

Stevie realized with a shock, except Carole. Carole stood alone by the water trough with a bucket in her hands, and she looked livid. Stevie blinked. She had never, ever, seen her friend so angry.

"Carole should have been more careful!" Amelia sobbed.

"More careful with what?" Max asked.

"She knocked that bucket over! She was telling me how Patch is scared of loud noises, and then she knocked the bucket off the fence, and Patch jumped and I was so-oo-o s-scar-ed!" Amelia broke into a torrent of fresh sobs. "I think she did it on purpose! She doesn't like me!"

Lisa couldn't believe her ears. Carole was never careless around horses, though even she sometimes had accidents. But Lisa knew for a fact that Carole hadn't dropped the bucket on purpose. She looked around the group of riders. "You know that isn't true," Lisa said. "Carole wouldn't do that to you, Amelia."

"Did anyone actually see what happened?" Max asked quietly. No one had.

"Max," Lisa said quickly, "you can't possibly believe—"

"Max," Stevie cut in urgently, "Carole would never, ever—"

"I was so scared!" Amelia wailed. "She did it on purpose. She doesn't like me, and she wanted to scare me."

"Carole, what happened?" Max asked.

Carole looked strangely pale. "I told her Patch spooked at

48

loud noises," she said, in an oddly tight voice. "And then—"

"Patch spooked! He nearly ran you over, Max! He's a bad, scary horse, and I don't want to ride him, not ever!"

Max looked as though he couldn't stand another second of hysteria. He stood up, patted Amelia absentmindedly, and looked around at his riders. "All right," he said, "let's put this behind us. Amelia, stop crying. Carole, I'd like to talk to you in my office in five minutes. Stevie, take that bucket from Carole and go get some more grain. We're going to have to catch those horses if we ever want to ride."

"Max—" Lisa said.

"Later, Lisa!"

"But Max—"

"Go get the grain, Stevie!"

When Max spoke like that, they knew better than to argue. Stevie gave Carole's hand a quick squeeze as she took the bucket from her. Carole looked at them all and lifted her chin. She hung Patch's lead rope and halter carefully on the fence, then walked slowly back into the stable. She didn't look at, or speak to, anyone.

Lisa's heart went out to her friend. Even though the stampede had been frightening, Amelia was blowing things way out of proportion. The little brat was just looking for an excuse not to ride Patch.

"Go get Barq, please, Lisa," Max directed wearily. Lisa

wanted to go after Carole instead. But what had Max said? He'd talk to Carole in five minutes. Everything would be cleared up then.

Lisa turned back to the pasture. "Just keep me away from that brat," Lisa whispered to Stevie, who had come back with more grain. "I might resort to violence."

"She's not Dr. Jekyll and Mr. Hyde," Stevie said in agreement. "She's Dr. Jekyll and the whole Hyde family, Hyde, Hyde, and Hyde Junior."

Lisa sighed. "How long is it until next Saturday?"

"Forever," said Stevie. "Forever."

6

"OKAY, ADAM, HERE'S Calypso for you," Lisa said, handing
the mare's lead rope to him. She shut the gate. It had only
taken a few minutes to round up all the horses and get them
to their riders, but to Lisa it felt like a few years. She
couldn't wait to talk to Carole.

Amelia hovered near Max's side. "Who am I going to ride
now, Max?"

Lisa looked at Stevie, who nodded and came over to her
side. "Are we finished?"

"I think so," Stevie said. "Except for Patch." They walked
closer to Max and Amelia.

"Patch will be okay now," Max was saying. "He settles down pretty quickly."

"But he's too scary! I can't ride him now, I'm too afraid!" Amelia again seemed on the point of tears. "Can't I ride Prancer?"

Max sighed. Lisa thought he was starting to look a little tired of Amelia. "I'll tell you what," he said. "Why don't you take Delilah instead of Patch? She's a very nice mare, and she's still in her stall, so you can go inside and start tacking her up right away."

"Is she like Prancer?" Amelia persisted.

"She's a palomino," Max said. "Her coat is golden blond, and her mane and tail are almost white. Her stall is the third one on the right, and her saddle, bridle, and grooming bucket are marked with her name in the tack room."

"Oh, I like palominos! Thank you, Max!" Amelia skipped into the stable.

" 'Is she like Prancer?' 'She's a palomino'?" Stevie repeated quizzically. "Max, that makes absolutely no sense. Prancer isn't a palomino."

"It seemed like the easiest answer to give," Max said. He shook his head ruefully. "What a ruckus. Let's go talk to Carole and get to the bottom of this."

To their surprise, Carole was not waiting in Max's office. Lisa and Stevie checked Starlight's stall and found the gelding alone, contentedly munching on a rack of new hay.

52

Carole's soaking bucket and package of salts had been cleared away, and all her grooming tools, which had been scattered across a hay bale in the aisle, were gone.

Lisa and Stevie met Max coming out of the tack room. "She's not with Starlight," Stevie said. "Did you check the locker room?"

"Yes, and she isn't there," Max said. "And her coat is gone and her cubby door is closed. But did you see this?" He pointed to the *brat* spelled out on the hat rack.

Stevie flinched. "I didn't do it, Max. I would have, but I didn't have time."

"I know you didn't," Max said grimly. "But you've spelled things in the past. I'm sure that's where Carole got the idea."

Lisa was horrified. "Oh, Max, Carole didn't do that! She wouldn't!"

"I agree, Lisa, it isn't like Carole at all," Max said. "Nor is it like her to spook a horse on purpose." He marched back to his office, and the girls followed him.

"You can't believe Carole did that," Stevie protested. "Max! This is Carole. Not me, not Veronica, *Carole*."

"I don't believe it." Max sat down in his chair and shook his head. "I know that had to have been an accident. But she really frightened Amelia—and no wonder—and she should at least apologize for that. Accidents happen, but I don't want Amelia becoming too afraid to ride."

53

"Max!" Lisa couldn't believe the way the conversation was heading. "Amelia is not going to be afraid. She's horrible, she always has to have her own way—"

"Did you see what happened?" Max asked.

"No," said Lisa. Stevie shook her head.

"You're forgetting that Amelia is only nine years old," Max said. "She's a little girl, and Lisa, I would expect you to show more patience toward your own cousin."

"I didn't ask for her to come here this week," Lisa said.

Max sighed. "As for Carole," he said, continuing as though Lisa hadn't spoken, "it bothers me that she left without talking to me first, especially after I asked her to stay. When you next talk to Carole, tell her that if she still wants to be an assistant instructor this week, all she has to do is apologize to Amelia, and we'll consider this whole incident over."

"Apologize to Amelia?" Stevie was astounded. "Max, you've got to be kidding!"

"Do you really mean Carole can't be an assistant instructor anymore?" Lisa asked. "That's not fair!"

"What if one of you kids had gotten hurt when the horses stampeded?" Max asked in return.

Lisa opened her mouth to protest further when Amelia's sweet voice trilled down the aisle: "Lisa? Can you help me? I found Delilah's saddle, but it's on one of the top racks and I can't reach it."

"Go on," Max said, with a wave of his hand. "Help her, and then you two tack up, too. We've had enough discussion. I'd like for you kids to ride sometime today."

Stevie let the door slam behind her as she and Lisa walked out. "I can't believe it!" she said.

"Neither can I," Lisa said. She was so upset that she was trembling. How could Max doubt Carole? It wasn't fair that Amelia should always get her own way! "I'll see you outside," Lisa told Stevie. "Tack up fast."

Stevie nodded. Every problem looked better from the back of a horse.

"HERE," LISA SAID, pulling Delilah's saddle off its rack and thrusting it roughly into Amelia's arms. She grabbed Prancer's bridle and slung her saddle over her arm.

"I found Delilah, and I groomed her and got her all ready except for the saddle," Amelia said cheerfully, following Lisa down the aisle. "She's very pretty, just like Max said."

Lisa didn't respond. She went into Prancer's stall and hugged the mare hard, breathing in her delicious horsey smell.

"Max said Delilah was every bit as good as Prancer," Amelia prattled on. "I agree. In fact, I think Delilah's better-looking."

Lisa began to curry Prancer with big, sweeping strokes. "Oh, certainly," she said, her voice heavy with sarcasm.

55

"Delilah, she's the number one horse in the stable. The absolute best. In fact, I'm sure she's a lot like Star the Wonder Horse at your stable. I can't believe Max is letting you ride her. You're really lucky, Amelia."

Delilah was a good mare with a lovely disposition, but she certainly wasn't the best horse in the stable. Thinking about it, Lisa realized that there probably was no "best" horse at Pine Hollow. They were all good at different things. Starlight could jump incredibly well, Calypso and Prancer both had fine pedigrees, Topside excelled at dressage. Tiny Quarter, one of the ponies, could jump a fence higher than his height, and he absolutely loved to be ridden cross-country. Old Patch was so sweet and careful that sometimes it seemed as if he, not Max, were teaching people how to ride. All these qualities were valuable. There was no one best horse any more than there was one best person at Pine Hollow.

Lisa leaned down until she was looking Amelia right in the eye. "If you don't tell Max the truth about that bucket, you're going to have a very long week," she said. "Now go tack up your horse, and leave me alone."

Amelia gave Lisa a small, slightly nervous smile. "But I did tell Max the truth about the bucket," she said. She trotted off to Delilah's stall. Lisa shook her head and turned back to Prancer.

* * *

56

ONCE SHE WAS in the saddle, Lisa's day started to improve. Prancer seemed to sense Lisa's mood and even seemed to be trying to cheer her up—the mare was being sweet and responsive. By the time they had jumped their first fence, Lisa felt much better. They flew over it with good style, and Lisa gave Prancer a pat.

"That was nice," Stevie whispered as Lisa got back in line.

"Thanks," Lisa whispered back. From the way the tense look had faded from Stevie's face, Lisa guessed that Stevie was also grateful to be riding. Best of all, Lisa reflected, they didn't have to deal with Amelia.

All the younger, less experienced riders had been put into a separate group, and Red was working with them on transitions. He was having them play a familiar game: When he said "Canter!" the last rider to canter had to stop and come into the center of the ring. In the end there was only one rider left. Lisa nearly fell off Prancer when she looked over and saw that it was Amelia.

"Look at her!" she said to Stevie, jerking her head in Amelia's direction. Red started the game over, with all the young riders at the rail. Amelia was much better than an average beginner. She kept her hands soft and her legs steady, and she was listening carefully to both Red and Delilah. Delilah, in turn, was listening to Amelia.

"She's an awfully considerate rider," Lisa said. Beginning

57

riders were often inconsiderate of their horses, not because they meant to be, but because they didn't yet have good balance and couldn't control their legs and hands well enough. Amelia seemed both balanced and gentle.

"I'm glad to see that she's considerate about something," Stevie snorted. Privately she thought that she had never met such a self-centered, manipulative whiner as Amelia. *And considering my brothers and their friends*, Stevie thought, *that's really saying something.*

By the time the lesson was over, Stevie and Lisa felt rejuvenated. As they walked their horses to cool them, they discussed what to do about Carole and Amelia.

"Poor Carole," Lisa said. "I mean, we can ride and feel better, but with Starlight lame she can't even do that."

"I don't want to upset you, Lisa, but I think this is more Amelia's fault than Carole's, no matter how the accident with the bucket happened." Stevie looked around. Amelia was walking Delilah near the Pony Tails and their ponies.

"Oh, I completely agree," Lisa said. "I'll make her shape up if I can. But whatever we do, we've got to fix things between Carole and Max."

"We need to talk to Carole," Stevie said.

"That's right," Lisa agreed. "We'll figure out something."

She looked toward Amelia and the Pony Tails again. "Are they arguing? I can't believe it!"

"I can," Stevie said.

AMELIA HAD RUN UP Delilah's stirrups and loosened her girth and was hand-walking her up and down the driveway. She passed the Pony Tails, who were walking their ponies the opposite way.

"You did well in our lesson," Corey said tentatively. "You won two times out of five."

Amelia smiled. "That's just because I was riding Delilah. She's such a nice horse, she makes everything easy."

"Good horses are like that," May said.

"Yep. It's too bad about your pony, Corey."

"What do you mean?" Corey asked.

"Well, I mean, he's so funny-looking," Amelia said. "And my cousin Lisa told me he was really strange."

Corey's mouth dropped open.

"He is *not* funny-looking," May retorted hotly. "*You're* funny-looking."

Amelia's eyes filled with tears, but then she blinked them back and took a deep breath.

"And I bet Lisa never said that," May continued.

"It doesn't matter," Amelia said calmly. "Anyway, Max gave me Delilah because he recognized what a superior rider I am, even though I haven't been riding as long as some people. My cousin Lisa said Delilah was the best horse in the barn and only very special people get to ride her."

"Oh, give me a break," Jasmine said. "You just make stuff up. Delilah is a great horse, but you don't have to be someone great to ride her. I rode her for my very first lesson ever."

Lisa walked up just in time to hear what Jasmine said. She sighed. She could guess that Amelia was bragging about herself, her riding skill, and her horses again, but she decided to ignore it. She'd been thinking during her lesson, and she'd decided that what she really needed to do was somehow inspire Amelia to behave. The problem was, she couldn't come up with anything inspirational to say.

To her amazement, Amelia turned on her before she could even open her mouth. "You lied to me!" Amelia said. "You said Delilah was a great horse, just like Star!"

"She probably is like Star," Lisa said. "And what difference does it make? You liked her, and you had a nice ride. And while we're on the subject of lying—"

"You're not nice, Lisa! I'm going to get you for this!"

"Oh, brother," Lisa said. "Who cares?"

"Not me!" Amelia pulled on the reins and led Delilah

into the stable. Lisa stared. After only one day in Amelia's company, she was entirely drained of energy.

Stevie walked up and shook her head. "Is she going to have to be a Saddle Club project?"

Lisa nodded. "Is she ever."

BY THE TIME Lisa got Prancer untacked and settled, her mother had arrived to drive her and Amelia home. Lisa was silent during the trip. She wanted to tell her parents all about Amelia's behavior, but she wasn't comfortable bringing it up in front of Amelia. The girl would probably start World War III, and Lisa didn't have the energy for combat just then.

She wished she'd had a moment to talk with Stevie before she left. She hadn't come up with any good ideas for dealing with Amelia, but Stevie's creativity could usually be counted on.

"I'm going to change," Amelia said, running up the stairs of Lisa's house. Lisa followed more slowly. Amelia shut the door of Lisa's room and locked it.

"Hey!" Lisa shouted. "Let me in!"

"I'm getting dressed!" Amelia called back.

"I want to change, too!" Lisa pounded on the door. "Let me in!"

"Just a minute!" Amelia shouted.

Lisa's mother came up the stairs with a basket of clean laundry. "Here," she offered, "take some clothes and use the bathroom. Don't worry about Amelia."

Lisa locked herself in the hall bathroom and yanked a clean sweatshirt over her head. If she found her reading her letters again, or messing with any of her stuff, Amelia was going to catch it good.

Lisa washed her hands and face and combed her hair. When she heard Amelia leave her room and go downstairs, she sighed with relief and began to plan. First she was going to tell her parents how Amelia had behaved in the pasture. Then she was going to call Carole. She went downstairs and poked her head into the living room to see if her mother was there.

Lisa gave a squeak of horror. Amelia was climbing onto the hobbyhorse!

"Get off that!" Lisa shouted. She rushed across the room

and grabbed Amelia, lifting her just as she was about to sit down. "I told you not to play with it! You'll break it." She tried to pull Amelia away.

Amelia resisted. "I want to! Leave me alone!"

"You can't!" Lisa said. "Nobody is allowed to play with it." She tugged at Amelia's arm, but Amelia tugged back. "It's made for really little kids," Lisa said. "You're too big."

"You just don't want me to play with it because you don't like me," Amelia retorted. "You don't want me to have any fun at all. You hate me!"

Lisa gave Amelia's arm another jerk. She was thoroughly fed up. "What do you expect?" she asked. "After the way you acted toward Carole, one of my best friends? After the way you talked to the Pony Tails? After the way you carried on about Prancer? You're the biggest brat I've ever met!"

Amelia let out an anguished howl and threw her weight backward, tearing herself out of Lisa's grasp. She stumbled against the hobbyhorse, and it crashed to the floor under her. "*Ow!*" Amelia cried.

Lisa rushed to Amelia's side, but she was much more concerned about the hobbyhorse. Sure enough, the worst had happened. One of the hobbyhorse's legs had snapped in two. "Now look what you've done!" she said.

"Did it really break?" Amelia asked, scrambling to her feet.

Lisa nodded. She touched the fresh, jagged edge of the

wood. "Right above the hock," she said, fighting back tears. The beautiful hobbyhorse! Lisa remembered the day they'd found it in an antiques store in London. She'd been so happy that her parents had bought it, and she'd loved it so much. She couldn't believe Amelia had broken it.

"Lisa! Amelia!" Mrs. Atwood came into the room. "What was all that noise and yelling?"

"Oh, Mom—" Lisa started to cry. So did Amelia.

"The horse broke!" Amelia sobbed. "We were playing, and Lisa pushed me, and the horse broke!"

"I did not!" Lisa said, through her tears.

"My arm hurts," said Amelia. "And the poor horse—"

"It was her fault, Mom—"

"It really hurts—"

"Girls!" Mrs. Atwood said sternly. "That's quite enough!"

"And it's broken!" Lisa wailed.

"That's enough! I can see that it's broken, Lisa. It's a real shame." She herded the girls into the kitchen.

Lisa expected a serious lecture about carelessness and destroying another person's property, with perhaps a sermon on the side about telling lies. Since she was always punished when she did something wrong, she was sure Amelia would be punished now. So would she, probably, since maybe she was partly to blame. If she had gotten Amelia away from the horse quickly enough, she might have prevented the accident.

65

But Lisa's mother didn't say a single word about the broken horse. She took a pot out of the cupboard and set it on the stove.

"Did my mom call yet?" Amelia asked softly.

Mrs. Atwood took out a packet of cookies. She gave two to Lisa and two to Amelia, then patted the younger girl's shoulder. "Not yet. I'm sure she knew how busy you'd be today. So tell me how you liked Pine Hollow."

Lisa didn't understand her mother's lack of reaction to the broken hobbyhorse. Was Mrs. Atwood simply too angry to discuss it? Was she feeling sorry for Amelia? Or did she really believe the accident was Lisa's fault? Lisa didn't know what to think. She crossed her arms and braced herself for Amelia's version of the day at Pine Hollow.

Amelia's sulky expression cleared. She smiled at her aunt. "Max is the nicest person," she began. "And so is Red. He taught my lesson. He was really good, and he said funny things, and he told me I did a good job on my walk-canter transitions. I rode Delilah. She's not the best horse, but she did okay."

"Sounds like you had fun," Mrs. Atwood said with a smile.

"Oh, I did! Pine Hollow is an awfully nice place, you know. They take really good care of the horses. You can tell by how happy the horses look."

Lisa blinked. Everything Amelia was saying was absolutely true, but it was only part of the truth. Amelia was giving Mrs. Atwood the Dr. Jekyll version of the day.

I should tell Mom the truth, Lisa thought. *I should tell her that Amelia lied and whined and cried, and that I can't stand being near her one second more.* But she felt too beaten down by the events of the day to say a single word.

"Lisa rode Prancer today, and they looked really good when they were jumping," Amelia continued. "They went over an oxer that was almost three feet high! Prancer looked great. I'm probably going to ride her on Monday." Amelia smiled sweetly at her cousin. "Lisa can ride Delilah."

"I'm going upstairs," Lisa said. She locked herself in her room and looked for evidence of Amelia's continued snooping. When she didn't find any, she took a blob of petroleum jelly and mixed it with some purple ink from her stamp pad. She smeared the mixture on the inner side of all her drawer handles. If Amelia opened any of them, she'd be caught purple-handed.

AT DINNER NOT a single word was said about the broken hobbyhorse. It had disappeared from the living room, and Lisa's parents seemed ready to pretend it had never existed at all. Lisa wanted to tell her side of the story, but she didn't. She knew how upset she would be if her parents believed Amelia instead of her. Lisa was already afraid that they did.

Finally, after dinner, she locked herself in her father's

study and conference-called Stevie and Carole. First she told them about the hobbyhorse. The rest of The Saddle Club was as upset as she was.

"I always liked to imagine that some fancy lord and lady had it made for their children," Carole said.

"They probably did," Lisa said. "When the kids outgrew the hobbyhorse, they were old enough for a real pony. And now it's ruined."

"The word *ruined* comes to mind when I think about today," Stevie said. "Amelia—well—"

"—should be kept in a zoo," Lisa finished.

"I wasn't going to say that," Stevie said, "but I agree. If you could find a zoo that would take her, that is."

"I don't know," Lisa said, relenting a little. "Sometimes I'm almost sorry for her. She looks like she doesn't know how to belong anywhere, except maybe on the back of a horse. But then she does something so awful, I can't be sorry for her. Carole, what happened today? Stevie and I were so worried about you. Are you okay?"

"We know you didn't do anything wrong," Stevie put in quickly. "You don't even have to explain."

"Thanks." Carole's voice quavered. "Wow, it was really a lousy day, wasn't it? I guess maybe I should have stayed and talked to Max—"

"He shouldn't blame you for anything, not for a second," Lisa said.

68

"—but I was just so upset," Carole continued. "If Starlight were sound I would have taken him on a trail ride, but since I couldn't, I just wanted to go home. I watched the video of *National Velvet* twice. It hardly helped at all. I didn't knock that bucket off the post, Lisa. Amelia threw it."

Stevie sucked in her breath.

"Oh, I can't stand her," Lisa said. "I should have known. It wasn't an accident at all."

"Max could have been killed," Stevie said.

"Or one of the horses could have been hurt," said Carole. "Especially Patch. I don't think Amelia knew what was going to happen, but that doesn't excuse her."

"No, it doesn't," Lisa said.

"The thing that upset me most, once I knew that Max was okay, is that all the little kids have always liked us before," Carole continued. "And at first I thought Amelia did, too, because she really seemed to listen to everything I told her about horses. That's part of why I thought this assistant instructorship was going to be so much fun—I like helping kids. I guess I like knowing they look up to me. So when Amelia accused me of spooking Patch—on purpose, no less—I was really shocked. I didn't even think about defending myself. I didn't think I had to."

"Max asked us to tell you that you can still be an assistant instructor," Lisa said reluctantly. "He said all you have to do is apologize to Amelia—not because you did anything wrong, Max knew better than that—but because your 'accident' frightened her."

There was a long pause. Stevie snorted.

"Please don't take any offense at this, Lisa," Carole said politely, "but I'd rather eat a bucket of live beetles than apologize to your cousin for something she did. Even being an assistant instructor isn't worth that. Amelia should be the one to apologize."

"I agree." Lisa felt miserable. "I don't blame you at all. It's just . . . tomorrow we're going to another relative's house, you know, so I won't be at Pine Hollow anyway. But Monday and all the rest of the week—especially with Amelia here—I don't know what Stevie and I will do without you. We'll miss you so much."

"Who says I won't be at Pine Hollow?" Carole was indignant. "I won't be an assistant instructor, that's all. Gosh, Lisa, Starlight's leg needs to be soaked twice a day! I went back to Pine Hollow this evening already to do it."

Carole felt a wave of grief wash over her. Starlight had seemed more lame than ever.

"I'm sorry," Lisa said. "Of course you'll be there. I wish so much that Starlight weren't hurt, but I'm glad you'll be around."

"Starlight will be okay," Stevie said. She had heard the misery in both her friends' voices. Stevie knew Lisa was upset about Amelia. Now Stevie thought about how upset Carole was over Starlight.

"You know, abscesses are pretty common," Stevie said. "I'm sure that's what it is. Starlight is going to be fine."

"I hope so." Carole's voice quavered. "I don't know. If it's navicular—Judy still hasn't been to see him. Some horse got tangled in a barbed-wire fence, and she spent the afternoon in surgery again. She says she'll be out as quickly as she can."

"It's the first time he's really been hurt," Lisa said soothingly, "so I'm sure you're worried. But most horses have little problems sometimes. He'll be okay."

"I don't know," Carole repeated. "There's no cure for navicular disease."

There was a moment of silence on the phone. "What do you mean, no cure?" Stevie asked hotly.

"It's a progressive condition, like arthritis," Carole said. "We could give him pain medicine, but we'd never be able to make him right." She bit her lip to keep from crying. "He'd never be able to jump again. He'd get worse and worse. Usually it happens in older horses, but sometimes young ones get it, too."

"He doesn't have it," Stevie said fiercely. "Not Starlight. I bet it's not even as serious as an abscess. I bet he just sprained his ankle a little, the way you did that one time getting out of the car."

71

"Whatever it is," Lisa said, "we'll help you in any way we can."

"Thanks," Carole said gratefully, after a pause. "I—I may really need you guys."

"And Lisa, we'll help with Amelia," Stevie promised. "We'll be at Pine Hollow on Monday when you get there."

"Thanks," Lisa said. "I don't know what I'd do without you two. Another day like today will do me in."

Lisa said good night and hung up the phone. She went upstairs. The door of her room was unlocked; inside, Amelia was already sound asleep in Lisa's bed. Lisa turned the closet light on so that she could find her pajamas. Amelia didn't stir. She snored more loudly than ever. Lisa crept to her cousin's side. Carefully she examined Amelia's hands for telltale purple marks. Amelia's fingernails were dirty, but that was all. Lisa looked at her own fingernails, which were also dirty. She guessed Amelia hadn't snooped yet.

Lisa dropped Amelia's hand back onto the bedcovers. Amelia didn't move. "If you can sleep this soundly," Lisa told her, "you don't need to worry about the guest room being scary. You won't be awake long enough to feel frightened."

Someone—Amelia?—had unrolled Lisa's sleeping bag at the foot of the bed, opened the zipper, and put Lisa's pillow at its head. Lisa grabbed her pillow and marched out. She would sleep in the guest room herself.

8

ON SUNDAY, LISA, her parents, and Amelia spent the day with Lisa's aunt and uncle. Fortunately they had three children younger than Amelia, so Superbrat bossed them around the whole day and ignored Lisa. Lisa curled up on her aunt's couch and read magazines. She was happy to be left alone.

Monday morning Amelia came down to the breakfast table in another new pair of jodhpurs and another tidy wool sweater. Her face was scrubbed clean, she'd polished her paddock boots, and she had tied bright ribbons at the ends of her braids.

"Why, Amelia," said Mrs. Atwood, "you look very nice."

73

"Thank you, Aunt Eleanor," Amelia said politely. "Could you please wash my other jodhpurs for me? They got a little dirty on Saturday." She slid into her chair and reached for the cereal.

"Of course. I must say, it's a pleasure having someone around who takes as much care with her appearance as you do." Lisa's mother gave Lisa a sideways smile, and Lisa sighed. She'd been wearing the same pair of breeches for three days now, and she hadn't cleaned her boots in more than a week. But she was wearing clean socks and a fresh shirt, her hair was clean and combed, and she'd brushed her teeth. She wasn't dirty. Besides, no one around the stable cared what she looked like. The only person who really fussed over her appearance was Veronica diAngelo.

"Do you think I look okay, Lisa?" Amelia asked shyly.

"Sure. Pass the orange juice, will you?"

A smile had started on Amelia's face, but it faded under the scornful tone in Lisa's voice. Amelia pushed the orange juice carton sullenly across the table, and it spilled a little.

"Be careful!" Lisa said.

"I'm *trying*."

Something anxious in the tone of Amelia's voice made Lisa look at her more closely. Was it possible that Amelia was worried about how she looked? Suddenly it occurred to Lisa that Amelia was just trying to look right, to fit in. She wanted to be liked. Unfortunately, Lisa thought with a sigh,

74

she also wanted to get her own way a hundred and six percent of the time.

On the way to Pine Hollow, Lisa thought sadly about the broken hobbyhorse. Her parents had still not said one word about it, so neither had she. She'd avoided going into the garage, because she didn't want to see the beautiful piece of art sitting on top of the trash.

Amelia didn't speak to Lisa after the exchange at the breakfast table. When they got out of the car at Pine Hollow and waved good-bye to Lisa's mother, Amelia turned to Lisa. "Can I ride Prancer today?" she asked.

"Don't be stupid," Lisa said crossly. "You're not going to ride her at all this week. I'm sure Max will give you Delilah again, and you ought to be happy with her. You got along fine with her Saturday." She didn't understand Amelia's obsession with riding Prancer, especially given how much fun she'd had with Delilah.

Amelia's eyes filled with tears. "But I don't want to ride Delilah. I want to ride Prancer."

Lisa shrugged. "Too bad." There were six more days until Amelia went home, and she was counting.

"*Ohh!*" Amelia stamped her foot and headed into the stable. Lisa went in search of her friends.

As she headed down the aisle, she saw the Pony Tails all vigorously grooming their ponies. "Hey, guys!" she called to them.

75

Corey looked up from currying Samurai. A funny expression passed over her face, and she went back to her grooming without saying a word.

"Hi, Corey," Lisa said again. "Is something wrong?"

Corey stared at a spot on Samurai's flank. "No," she said.

Lisa frowned. *What was that about?* As she continued down the aisle, she heard May saying, "I'm telling you, Corey, Lisa never said anything bad about Sam . . ."

She sighed. Amelia again, she was sure of it. She started to turn back to talk to the younger girls, but Stevie poked her head out of Starlight's stall and called for her.

"What's wrong?" Lisa asked. Both Carole and Stevie were standing anxiously by Carole's horse.

"Nothing," Stevie said. "We just wanted your opinion. Feel here." She lifted Starlight's lame foot and pointed to a spot on the hoof.

"That's strange," Lisa said, feeling carefully. "It feels hot." She bent and felt the same spot on Starlight's other front foot, for comparison. The gelding nuzzled her hair. "It definitely feels hot."

"We think so, too," Stevie said. "See, Carole, it is an abscess. That spot'll open up, drain, and heal."

Carole patted her beloved horse sadly. "I hope so."

Lisa shuddered. " 'Open up' sounds awful."

Carole closed her eyes as if she were feeling Starlight's pain.

"It won't be awful at all," Stevie said cheerfully. "Judy'll just make a tiny hole to let the infection out. Starlight will feel a lot better then."

Unless it's navicular, Carole thought. *Maybe navicular made horses' hooves feel hot, too.* She moaned.

"It'll be okay," Stevie said reassuringly. "He's going to be fine."

Carole laughed a little shakily. "I know, Stevie, but if it were Belle—"

"—I'd be feeling awful, and you'd be saying, 'Stevie, she's going to be fine,'" Stevie finished for her. They all laughed.

"I'm going to wait to soak his foot until you guys are riding," Carole said. "It'll give me something to do. Say, Lisa, where's Amelia?"

"Who cares?" Lisa asked.

"Well," Stevie said, "it's probably better to keep an eye on her."

"You're right," Lisa said gloomily. "She's probably telling the Pony Tails about her wonder horse, Star. Or else she's mooning over Prancer. Let's go get her."

Amelia wasn't with the Pony Tails or in Prancer's stall. The Saddle Club peeked into Belle's stall, too, and Delilah's, but didn't find her. Quite a few of the other riders had arrived for camp, and the stable was full of busy people, but they didn't see Amelia anywhere.

As they approached the locker room, Lisa heard Amelia

talking inside. She held up her hand to silence her friends, and the three girls crept closer to the open door.

"See, I'm just going to go get Prancer and I'm going to ride her," she was saying. "Once Max sees how well I do with her, he'll let me keep riding her. Don't you think so, Veronica?"

"Um," they could hear Veronica say. "I don't know. I think perhaps you're overestimating Prancer. She's a nice-looking horse, but of course she can't be that valuable, or Max wouldn't let Lisa ride her. And she behaved very badly at a horse show once. Not like my Danny. Now there's a horse."

"Prancer's a registered Thoroughbred," Amelia said.

"Umm, yes, of course she is," Veronica said. "Step aside, Amelia. I need to put on my good boots. Did you happen to notice them the other day? They're custom-made—the very finest."

"I'm going to get boots soon," Amelia said. "And I'm *not* riding Delilah today."

Lisa started to walk into the locker room. She'd heard quite enough. Amelia continued, "I'm having a miserable vacation, and it's all Lisa's fault." Lisa froze. Stevie and Carole bumped into her, then stopped, too. "If Lisa had acted nice to me, then Stevie and Carole and everybody else would have liked me, and then I could have ridden Prancer

78

yesterday instead of Delilah," Amelia said. "Don't you think so, Veronica?"

"Umm . . . maybe." Veronica sounded distracted, as if she wasn't listening. "Look at this mud on my boots! I told our handyman to be sure to get the heels clean this time!"

Max walked up behind The Saddle Club just in time to hear Amelia say, "So I'm just going to go ride Prancer right now."

"You can't do that," Veronica said. "You're too little. Really, it's a bad idea. It would be dangerous."

"Amazing," Stevie whispered. "Veronica, doing the right thing?"

Carole shook her head. "She's a jerk, but she does know about horses. She knows Amelia would get hurt."

"I'll stop this," Max said quietly. He started to walk into the room, but Amelia had already said, "Yes! I'm going to! I'm tired of people telling me what to do!"

"No, you can't! I'll tell Max!" Veronica said.

"*Ahhhh!*" The Saddle Club heard a terrific crash.

"Stop that! My boots!" Veronica shouted furiously. Something else crashed. Max and The Saddle Club rushed into the locker room just as one of Veronica's expensive boots came flying out the door.

Amelia had thrown herself into a complete tantrum. She grabbed a box of hair supplies out of Veronica's cubby and hurled it after Veronica's boot. Before Max could reach her, she flung herself down on the floor, sobbing incoherently and kicking her feet like a two-year-old.

"Quiet!" Max roared. He hauled her to her feet. Amelia subsided into whimpering moans. "I said *quiet!*" She quit crying and gave Max a sulky look.

She doesn't even look ashamed, Lisa thought in amazement.

"Veronica, go check on Danny for a moment," Max said. Veronica left in a flash, her eyebrows raised in disdainful astonishment. "Now, Amelia"—he put his face very close to hers—"if you *ever* want to ride here again, you will quit blubbering, wash your face, and report to my office in exactly two minutes. Now, scoot!" He gave her a little push out the door.

"As for you three . . ." Max straightened and suddenly looked weary. "Let's go to my office."

9

STEVIE, CAROLE, AND LISA slowly filed into Max's office. Lisa felt drained. Just witnessing Amelia's tantrum had sucked all the energy out of her. She would not be able to stand six more days of this. Max shut the door behind him, and they all looked at one another awkwardly.

"Please sit down," Max said. "You didn't drop that bucket, did you?" he asked Carole.

She shook her head.

"Did Amelia throw it, by any chance?" he continued. Carole looked miserable. Finally she nodded.

"I owe you an apology. It looks like I misjudged the situation with Patch and Amelia. Will you please forgive me?" He solemnly held out his hand.

Carole shook it. To her surprise, tears came to her eyes. She felt so relieved.

Max looked around the room. "Lisa, Stevie, I should have listened to you, too. I'm very sorry."

"It's okay, Max," Lisa said softly. She felt heartsick that things had gone this far. They sat in silence for a few moments, until Amelia knocked and came in.

Her eyes were still red from crying, but she had washed her face, brushed the dirt off her sweater, and retied the ribbons on her braids. "Max," she said, as soon as she came into the room, "I'm very, very sorry for everything I did. I promise I'll be much better, if only you let me ride again." She smiled at him beseechingly. Her lower lip trembled.

Max didn't smile back. "You should apologize to Stevie and Lisa and Carole," he said. "Especially to Carole."

Amelia turned and held her hands out to Carole. "I'm very sorry. I shouldn't have said that about you."

"You should apologize to Patch," Carole said. "You scared him."

Amelia nodded. "Okay, I will. Lisa, Stevie, I'm sorry, okay?" She turned to Max. "Now can I ride again? Please?"

"Why did you throw the bucket that spooked Patch?" Max asked.

82

Tears filled Amelia's eyes, and one ran down her cheek. "I didn't know he would act like that," she said. "I thought he would just jump a little. I didn't mean for all the horses to run! I'm sorry. I just didn't want to ride Patch."

"Patch is a good horse," Max said firmly.

"I'm really sorry," Amelia said.

Max drew in a heavy breath. "It's not as easy as that," he said. "Sometimes apologies are not enough. I misjudged The Saddle Club here, especially Carole, and I should not have, so I need to do something to make it up to them. They had earned my trust, and I should have trusted them.

"Riding is a privilege, not a right," he continued. "Especially, riding at my barn is a privilege, and privileges, like trust, are something you earn.

"I should kick you out, Amelia. You scared Patch on purpose, and you were planning to ride a horse without my permission. Both of those are dangerous and should be enough to end your riding privileges here. But, as I said, I owe something to The Saddle Club, too."

He sat back in his chair, and Carole thought she could detect a glint of satisfaction in his eyes. "I'm letting The Saddle Club decide your fate, Amelia. If they think you shouldn't be allowed to ride here, you won't be."

"OUT!" STEVIE SAID as she sat down on a tack trunk. "Out, out, out!" She cackled with glee.

"Well . . . ," Carole said hesitantly, sitting down beside Stevie. They were in the tack room, where they'd gone for privacy while they discussed Amelia's fate.

"I wouldn't have to deal with her for the whole week," Lisa said, leaning back against the wall and closing her eyes. "It would be so wonderful. I don't know what Amelia would do by herself—but I guess that isn't my problem, is it? My mom could take her shopping, or they could go to museums. Anywhere, so long as she isn't here. It would be heaven."

"It would be awful for Amelia," Stevie said with satisfaction. "A week of shopping and museums—the perfect revenge!"

"It *would* be awful," Lisa said. "Too awful. I don't know. I don't want her around, but I'm not sure that that's reason enough to ban her. I didn't want her here in the first place, and I think—I think I could have been nicer to her."

"What she did was horrid," Carole said. "I don't mean lying about me, although that was bad enough. Poor Patch! And remember, Max almost got killed."

"She didn't know the horses would stampede," Stevie pointed out. "She said so, and I believe her. She's not *that* bad. She's just a little kid, and she didn't know what would happen."

"I believe her, too, but she's the same age as the Pony Tails," Carole said indignantly. "They're very responsible."

"Yeah," Stevie said, "but Amelia really hasn't been around horses for very long."

"So you think we should let her keep riding?" Lisa asked.

"Not at all," Stevie said cheerfully. "All I said was that she wasn't trying to kill Max. She was definitely trying to scare Patch, and she definitely told lies, and she probably would have climbed on Prancer and had a horrible stupid accident. Plus, I'd rather not have her around."

"Max is right that riding is a privilege," Carole said. "I guess—I mean, she *should* be punished—"

"I think that's why she's such a brat," Lisa said. "She never has to take responsibility for what she does. Nobody makes her. When she ripped my books up three years ago, nobody made her say she was sorry. She broke our hobbyhorse, and my parents are acting as if nothing happened. She whines and throws a fit, and boom! she gets whatever she wants. So she keeps whining and throwing fits. I think she thinks that if she just keeps pushing for it, she'll get to ride Prancer, too."

"So you think that this time she ought to be punished," Carole said.

"Yes," said Lisa. "I do."

Carole sighed. "So do I."

"So we're in agreement," Stevie said. "She can't ride at Pine Hollow."

The three girls looked at each other. "That's right," said Lisa. "Only . . ."

"Only what?"

Lisa made a face. "It's hard to explain. She did do all these things she shouldn't have, and I think she should be punished, only . . . Did you hear what she said to Veronica in the locker room?"

" 'I'm just going to go ride Prancer right now?' " Stevie asked. "I heard that."

Lisa smiled but shook her head. "I mean when she said, 'I'm having a miserable vacation, and it's Lisa's fault. If she had been nice to me, everyone else would have liked me.' "

"What about it?" Stevie asked. "It's not even true. You did warn us about what a brat she was, but it wouldn't have taken us long to figure it out on our own. I personally don't think I would have liked her anyway."

"Except that I shouldn't have told you she was a brat," Lisa said. She looked down at the ground. "I knew she was a brat the last time I saw her, but that was three years ago. People change a lot in three years."

"Please," Stevie said. "She's still a brat, Lisa. You can't deny it."

"I know, but right from the start, I haven't been nice to her. At home, I mean. And when I brought her here, I didn't act like she was somebody special, like I really wanted you guys to meet her. I can tell she wants to have friends, but I didn't help her make friends at all, and I think I should have." Lisa sighed. "The truth is, I was pretty annoyed about having her come during my vacation. I'm a lot nicer to all the Pony Tails than I am to my own cousin."

"The last I checked," Stevie said, "the Pony Tails weren't mouthing off to you because Max wouldn't give them the horse they wanted."

"The Pony Tails have their own ponies," Lisa said. "Amelia and I don't. I know she can't ride Prancer, and I don't think she should, but I do know what it's like to want to have one special horse."

"So you think we should let her off the hook?" Stevie asked. "Pretend none of this happened, just like with the hobbyhorse?"

"No. . . . I don't know. I just don't know." Lisa sighed. "I didn't expect this to be so confusing!"

"Stevie," Carole said softly, "you've been in trouble a few times yourself—"

"A few hundred," Stevie said with a laugh.

"If you were Amelia, wouldn't you want a second chance?" Carole continued. "I bet she'd behave better now. And Lisa's right, you know, we were all expecting her to be a brat. If she were a horse and she misbehaved, we wouldn't just punish her. We'd try to correct her." Carole thought about the enormous patience that horse training required. Probably rider training took the same amount of work.

Stevie shook her head ruefully. "I can't believe that you two are passing up the one perfect chance to get Amelia out of our lives. Wait. No, I can believe it. And you're right, Carole, Max has given me lots of second chances.

"Besides," she added, "you almost lost your assistant instructor job over this. If you want to let Amelia keep riding, I'll go along."

"Me too." Lisa put out her hand and pulled Stevie to her feet.

WHEN THEY WALKED back into Max's office, Lisa was surprised to see that Amelia's face was deathly pale. She jumped to her feet when they came in and stared at them with wide, anxious eyes.

Max smiled. "Well?"

Lisa nodded. "We all agreed. As long as she behaves from now on, she can still ride."

Amelia blinked hard. "Thanks," she said, moving shakily toward the door. Her eyes widened, and she struggled not to cry. Suddenly Lisa had the feeling that these tears were more real than any of the others Amelia had shed recently. "Thanks very much," Amelia said. She wiped the back of her hand across her eyes and tried to smile nonchalantly.

"I'd better go saddle up, since I'm riding. Delilah, right, Max?"

"Wait a minute," Max said. He gave The Saddle Club a proud smile and put his arm around Carole's shoulder. "Amelia," he said, "meet Carole, my assistant instructor. I'm putting her in charge of you."

10

"Okay," Carole said, "first you go for the big piles." She leaned over the door of Delilah's stall. Behind her, Stevie and Lisa suppressed giggles. The first part of each day of camp was called stable management—a fancy name for manure mucking, tack cleaning, and all the other chores done around a stable. Amelia was the only camper who had never cleaned a stall before. The big pitchfork looked awkward in her small hands.

"Be careful not to get the wheelbarrow too full," Carole cautioned. "It'll be too heavy for you to push it. You're going to have to make several trips."

"Oorgh," Amelia muttered. Her pitchfork tilted, and its

90

contents dropped back onto the stall floor. "I can't do this!" she cried in frustration.

"Of course you can," Carole said cheerfully. "Look at it this way: It'll build up your arm muscles, and that's great for riding."

"It's hard," Amelia said.

"Well," Carole said, "it is hard, but you're doing a super job. Delilah will be much happier with a clean stall."

Amelia straightened and put her hands on her hips. "I hope so. Is this really part of camp, or is this part of my punishment? Because it seems like punishment. It even smells like punishment."

Stevie snorted and Lisa rolled her eyes.

"It's really part of camp," Carole said mildly. "Not only that, it's part of life. Every rider needs to know how to take care of her horse, and keeping its stall clean is the first step. I cleaned Starlight's before you got here this morning—and I know that when you get a horse of your own, you'll want to take really good care of it. Besides, if you don't do stable management here at camp, you don't ride."

Carole smiled, even though she didn't feel like it. She hadn't expected Amelia to be thrilled about cleaning Delilah's stall, but she had hoped that maybe she would be able to work a little faster. Now that Carole was back to being Max's assistant, she had a lot to do, and she still had to soak Starlight's sore foot. She looked at her watch worriedly.

Stevie saw and immediately understood. "Hey, Assistant Instructor," she said. "What if Lisa and I become assistant's assistants? We'll help Amelia here while you go take care of Starlight."

"Thanks," Carole said. "It's only for fifteen minutes—Amelia won't be done with the stall yet . . ." She hurried off.

"I'm glad you thought of that," Lisa told Stevie, as they took up Carole's position by the stall door. "I know Carole's worried, but I've been so"—she glanced at Amelia—"preoccupied lately, I haven't been much help."

"She still thinks it's navicular," Stevie said in an undertone. "I hope Judy can come today."

"We'll keep our fingers crossed," Lisa said. "Poor Starlight!"

"Out of my way, please." Amelia had filled the wheelbarrow three-quarters full and pushed it to the door of the stall. Lisa scooted to one side, and Stevie held the door open. Amelia struggled to steer the barrow without overturning it.

"Hey, that's pretty full," Lisa said. "I bet it's heavy, and your arms are short. Why don't you let me take it outside?"

"I can do it," Amelia said. "I'm strong enough." She made a tremendous effort and got the wheelbarrow rolling down the aisle.

Lisa shook her head.

"She's tough enough, anyway," Stevie remarked. "I'd like

92

to see her take on my brother Chad. I bet she'd win." When Amelia came back with the empty wheelbarrow, a scowl still on her face, Stevie added, "You know, Amelia, this honestly isn't punishment. Everyone works at Pine Hollow."

Amelia wielded the pitchfork with vigor. "I don't mind working, but I'm behind everybody else," she said. "The Pony Tails are already finished with their stalls. They're in the tack room. They're telling jokes."

"They're cleaning their saddles," Lisa told her. "That's what you'll be doing as soon as you're done here."

"By then they'll probably be riding," Amelia said.

"Probably," said Stevie.

Lisa shot Stevie a look. "They won't start the lesson without you," she assured her cousin. Amelia looked relieved.

After Amelia's third wheelbarrow load, Stevie and Lisa declared the stall clean enough. "Good," said Amelia, dusting her hands on the seat of her jodhpurs and heading for the tack room.

"Not so fast," Stevie said, grabbing her shoulder. "You took three loads of dirty sawdust out, so you've got to put three loads of clean sawdust back in." She pointed down the aisle. "The sawdust pile is next to the grain room. Use a shovel instead of a pitchfork. It'll go faster."

Amelia grunted as she grabbed the empty wheelbarrow. Lisa and Stevie watched her march down the aisle. "Think I should clean Delilah's water bucket for her?" Stevie asked.

"No way," Lisa replied. "She's not being punished. She'd have to do this work whether she'd gotten in trouble or not."

"I know," Stevie said. "But the fact is, she is a lot slower than the rest of the campers, just because she's never done this stuff before. If we helped just a little, she'd be even."

"Stevie!" Lisa burst out laughing. "One minute you want to kick her out of the stable entirely, and the next you want to do her work for her. I said I'd try to be nicer to her, and I will, but she needs to do this herself."

Stevie grinned. "You're right. Only the faster she gets done, the sooner we can go ride!" They'd agreed to take a trail ride while Carole helped Max teach the morning camp lesson.

Stevie was demonstrating how to properly fluff the new bedding in Delilah's stall when Carole came back. She paused in the aisle to hug Delilah, who was waiting patiently on cross-ties for her stall to be cleaned. "Good old girl," Carole murmured soothingly. She had always loved Delilah.

"You know," she said to Amelia, "besides Starlight, of course, Delilah is my favorite horse at Pine Hollow. I rode her for years, starting when I first came here. You should be glad to ride her. A horse doesn't have to be high-strung and have a fancy pedigree to be good. I always knew that Delilah would try to do anything I asked. You can't expect a horse to be better than that."

Amelia shrugged. "Prancer is prettier. Her legs are longer, and her face is nicer."

Lisa sighed. Max had told Amelia in front of all of them that she would not ride Prancer this week and that she was not likely to ride a horse like Prancer for years. He had told her that she would ride Delilah for the rest of the week, without complaining, or she wouldn't ride at all. Amelia hadn't complained.

"Prancer and Delilah are just very different," Carole explained patiently. "Prancer's a Thoroughbred. Delilah is mostly quarter horse. Why are you so sure you'd like Prancer better, anyway?"

Amelia pressed her lips together, which made her look pouty. "Lisa rides Prancer," she said at last, without looking at her cousin.

"Ohhh," Carole said, in an understanding tone. She glanced at Lisa. "And you want to be like Lisa."

Amelia shrugged. "Not really." She looked up at Lisa, then continued, "My mom said that Lisa was riding a Thoroughbred, a very valuable horse. She thought it was really neat. So I thought she'd like it if I rode Prancer, too."

Lisa felt a sudden rush of sympathy for her. To Amelia, riding Prancer must have been like having fancy jodhpurs—a status symbol. "Whether a horse is valuable or not isn't an important thing about riding," she said. "The best horses aren't always the fancy ones, and the best riders are the ones who really love it."

"I know," Amelia said. "But my mom doesn't."

"Hey," Stevie reminded her, "don't you ride a pretty fancy horse at home anyway? You were telling us all about her."

"Star," Lisa remembered. "Star the Wonder Horse."

Amelia scowled harder than ever. "She's just a normal horse. I just happen to like her, that's all." She turned to Carole. "Aren't I supposed to be cleaning tack?"

"Sure," Carole said. Directing a roll of her eyes to her two friends, she led Amelia down to the tack room.

"I guess that means we put the wheelbarrow away," Stevie remarked. "And it looks like I'll be cleaning the water bucket, after all. Just this once, of course."

"Your wish come true," Lisa said jovially. "You get to do something for Amelia after all. But wasn't that weird? Star isn't so amazing after all. She's just a good, honest horse."

"Did you expect anything different?" Stevie asked.

"No," Lisa admitted. "What surprises me is that Amelia knew the truth all along. I always thought her instructor had convinced her that Star was really special. I never guessed that Amelia was trying to convince us—and her mother, I suppose. My aunt Marianne can be strange sometimes. She's like my mother, only much worse."

Stevie nodded understandingly. Lisa's mother's preoccupation with high society wasn't all bad—Mrs. Atwood had urged Lisa to start riding because it was something she thought all well-bred young ladies should do—but it was sometimes annoying for Lisa.

"I agree that your cousin is a constant surprise," Stevie said. "What I don't understand is why we're standing around talking about her when we could be out riding our horses and talking about her."

Lisa grinned. "Good point."

MOST OF THE young campers had gathered in the tack room by the time Amelia and Carole got there. They greeted Amelia in a much friendlier way than they had the day before. Carole guessed from the look on the Pony Tails' faces that the news of Amelia's tantrum had spread, and she was equally sure that the Pony Tails somehow knew the rest of the story: that Amelia was still allowed to ride, but only if she shaped up. All the younger riders looked ready to give Amelia a second chance, and Carole felt grateful to them. The people at Pine Hollow really were friendly.

"Hello, Amelia," Corey said softly.

Amelia looked at the floor. "Which tack do I clean, Carole?" she asked. Carole took Delilah's bridle off its peg and handed it to her. "Can you show me how?" she whispered, looking embarrassed. "At my stable—at home they don't show us how to do any of this."

Those were almost the only words Amelia spoke while she cleaned her tack. The rest of the kids laughed and chattered, asked Carole questions, and talked about their ponies, but Amelia sat silently, scrubbing at the pieces of Delilah's bridle as Carole directed her. The only time she talked at all was when Carole made her scrape the green crust off Delilah's bit with her fingernail.

"This is *disgusting*," she said.

"That's because you didn't wipe it off after you rode her the last time," May piped up helpfully. "She probably had some chewed-up hay in her mouth, and it got on the bit and dried there overnight."

Amelia hunched her shoulders. "Poor Delilah," she said.

"Hey, it's okay," May said. "You're cleaning it now, before she has to wear it."

Carole noticed that Amelia worked until the bit was sparkling clean.

Max stuck his head in the tack room door. "Anyone here want to ride?" he asked.

"Yeah!" all the kids chorused, as they grabbed their clean tack and trooped out the door. Amelia remained with Carole.

"I haven't cleaned my saddle yet," she said.

"That's okay," Carole assured her. "It's not very dirty, and you can do it later today." She helped Amelia balance the saddle on her arm. "Do you need me to help you tack up?"

"No thanks. They teach us *some* things at my other stable, you know." Amelia headed down the aisle.

Carole sighed, then went to pat Starlight before checking to make sure that Amelia had done it right.

BEING AN ASSISTANT instructor became much more fun the moment Carole took her place in the center of the riding ring next to Max. Eight small riders on horses or ponies circled the ring at a walk. Carole surveyed them all critically, mentally noting errors of position or control.

"Speak up," Max told her, looking down at her with a grin. "You go ahead and get them started. I'll add what I think."

"Okay," Carole said with a nervous grin. This was fun! "Everybody walk on. And May," she commanded, in a voice that carried across the arena, "you need to relax your hands a little. Let Macaroni get warmed up before you try to collect him. Joey, push Nickel on. He's being lazy. Excellent job with Penny, Jessica, but try to put more of your weight in your heels." She looked up at Max, who smiled and nodded; then she turned her attention back to the class.

"Amelia, squeeze with your legs to encourage Delilah to

99

go forward." Carole knew Delilah sometimes started out slowly. Amelia squeezed, and when Delilah didn't immediately respond, she clucked to the horse encouragingly. "That's right, Amelia! Good job!"

Carole went through the rest of the class, gently correcting and encouraging the kids. She was careful not to tell them to change too many things at once, and she tried to give them lots of praise. That was how Max had taught her. She knew how nice it felt to be told you were doing something right.

"Okay, everybody into the jump position, and trot." Max always had them do this at the start of the lesson. In the jump position, the rider stood slightly in the saddle. This took the rider's weight off the horse's back and gave the horse a chance to warm up thoroughly. It also encouraged the rider to use good leg position, which warmed up the rider.

"Grab the mane if you have to, Sarah. That's right. Keep your eyes straight ahead, Corey, and look through your turns. Good! Back straight, Jasmine. Great job! Doesn't that feel better?" Jasmine nodded, smiling. "Keep your chin up, Amelia. Good!"

Carole took them through several exercises at the posting and sitting trots, with Max adding his suggestions and comments as the class went along. Carole loved watching the kids improve under her teaching, and she would have been having a wonderful time if, in the back of her mind, she hadn't been worried about Starlight.

"Go ahead and tell them to canter," Max said quietly.

"All canter!" Carole told the group.

Neither Carole nor Max understood what happened next. Amelia gave Delilah a soft, correct canter signal, and Delilah leaped into the canter with a giant buck. Amelia sailed over Delilah's head and landed flat in the arena sand.

She didn't move or cry. While the other riders brought their mounts to a halt, Max and Carole hurried to Amelia's side.

The little girl looked up at them with wide, unblinking eyes.

"Are you okay?" Carole asked anxiously. She knew that most falls didn't do more than shake the rider up, but they were still scary. Most kids cried hard when they fell off. Amelia's silence worried her.

"Yes." Amelia got slowly to her feet with Max's help. He asked her several quick questions—"Does your head hurt?" "Are you dizzy?"—before seeming satisfied that she was okay.

Amelia looked up at Carole. "What did I do wrong?" she asked. "Does Delilah hate me?"

11

"OF COURSE SHE doesn't hate you. And you didn't do a single thing wrong," Carole said. She put her arm around Amelia. "I promise." She looked up at Max, who smiled sympathetically; then Carole took Amelia's hand and led her over to Delilah. The mare was standing at the side of the ring, her reins dangling. She looked sorry. Carole gathered Delilah's reins and handed them to Amelia. "Have you ever fallen off before?" she asked.

Amelia shook her head.

"Everyone does," Carole said.

"I know," Amelia whispered. "But it was scary. Why did Delilah do that?"

"I don't know," Carole said honestly. "She's probably just feeling her oats. She's a horse. No one understands horses all the time."

Amelia looked up at the palomino mare. Cautiously she touched Delilah's nose. "Am I still allowed to ride?" she asked.

"Of course," Carole said. "The lesson isn't over."

"Good." Amelia looped the reins over Delilah's neck. "Could you give me a leg up?"

"Sure." Carole boosted her into the saddle. She tried not to show how pleased she was that Amelia was getting right back on. Carole had known beginners who were so upset by their first fall that they gave up riding entirely.

Amelia's second attempt at a canter was a success. The girl looked nervous, but she still rode gently, and Delilah behaved well.

"Good job!" Carole said.

"Okay," Max said. "Let's do a little jumping." He set up two pole standards in the center of the ring.

"Max!" Carole whispered, going to help him with the jump. "Are you serious? Amelia will feel so left out."

"Why?" Max grinned. "She's going to be jumping, too."

Carole looked at him. She could hardly believe it. Amelia, jumping after only four months! But on the other hand, Lisa had started jumping just as quickly, and so had she. And Amelia was a good rider. "She'll love it," she whispered.

"I hope so," said Max.

He set up a small cross rail with several poles spaced evenly on the ground in front of it. "Now, I want you to come through this one at a time," he instructed the riders. "Go deep around the corner, get straight to the fence, and maintain an even pace throughout. Amelia, is this your first jump?"

Amelia's face was a mixture of nervousness and excitement. "Yes," she said.

"Then you go last, and watch the others. You should just concentrate on trotting Delilah exactly toward the center of the fence. Look over it, not at it. As you turn the corner, get into your two-point position, just as we practiced, and right before the fence, reach up and grab a handful of Delilah's mane. She'll do the rest. She knows all about jumping."

"Okay." Amelia took her place at the end of the line of riders.

"Come ahead, Jasmine," Carole called. "Keep your heels down. Keep Outlaw steady. Good!"

One by one the kids jumped the fence. Joey lost his balance and had to catch himself on Penny's mane, but everyone else jumped smoothly. They had all jumped before.

"Okay, Amelia," Max said.

"Okay," Amelia echoed. She gathered her reins and clucked to Delilah, who set off obligingly at a nice steady trot. Amelia guided her around the corner of the ring and headed her in a straight line toward the small fence.

Delilah tossed her head down, kicked her hind heels up, and jumped sideways. Amelia fought to keep her balance.

"Whoa!" commanded Max.

"Sit up!" yelled Carole. "Pull her head up!"

Amelia did all three and then added something on her own. She sat up, pulled Delilah's head back up, and told the horse, "Steady." Then she squeezed with her legs to make Delilah go forward. Delilah tossed her head. Amelia corrected her gently. With steely-eyed determination, she headed the horse straight for the fence. Delilah settled herself and jumped it.

Amelia brought Delilah to a controlled halt afterward, just as Max had told them all to do. "Way to go, Amelia!" May shouted, and the rest of the riders broke out in cheers.

When Carole reached Delilah's side, she saw that Amelia was grinning from ear to ear. It was the first time that she'd seen Amelia look genuinely happy, she realized with a start.

"You did it," Carole said. "Well done."

Amelia patted Delilah's neck over and over again. "I did, I really did!" she said. "I really jumped! Wait till my mom hears this!" To Max she added, "I think I know what's get-

105

ting her upset. The sun is making a funny reflection off the side mirror on that truck over there. I think Delilah's just tall enough so it hits her right in the eyes."

Carole ducked through the fence and adjusted the mirror. "Good thinking," Max told Amelia. "I like the fact that you looked for a reason for Delilah to spook. She doesn't usually, so you're probably right about the mirror. I also really, really, liked the way you dealt with her and still took the jump. You're a good rider, Amelia."

Amelia beamed. "Can we jump it again?" she asked. "I mean, may we? Please?"

The whole group jumped the fence five more times before Max called it quits. Delilah didn't spook again. "If Amelia smiles any harder, her lips are going to cramp," Carole told Max.

"Can you remember your first jump?" Max asked Carole.

Carole laughed. "Yes. My lips probably did cramp."

AS THEY WERE walking back into the stable, Max slapped his hand against his forehead. "Carole, I forgot!" he said. "Judy came here this morning to see Starlight, really early. She left a note for you in the office, but all it says is to call her. She wants to talk to you about him."

Happiness drained out of Carole like water out of a bathtub. "Did she say what was wrong with him?" Carole asked.

Max shook his head. "I wasn't here yet. Red let Judy in.

I'm sorry I didn't tell you sooner. But you can use the office phone to call her."

Carole went into the office and carefully shut the door. Her hands were shaking. She looked at the phone for a long time before she dialed Judy's number. If it were something minor, Judy would have said so in her note. It had to be something bad. Navicular disease. Carole was sure.

She dialed Judy's number by heart. The answering machine picked up. "Judy?" Carole said. "This is Carole. I'm calling from Pine Hollow. Please call when you can." She set down the phone and went in search of Lisa and Stevie.

She found them in the tack room, cleaning their saddles after their trail ride.

"Hey," Lisa said instantly. "Why are all the campers giving Amelia high fives in the aisle? We asked, and she just smiled. What happened in that lesson? She looks like an actual human being."

"She fell off Delilah, for starters."

"Is she hurt?" Lisa asked.

"No—"

"Hysterical?"

Carole grinned despite herself, remembering the lesson. "No, she was very calm, and she got back on and started jumping."

"Jumping?" Lisa asked. "Honestly?"

"Honestly," Carole said. "Six cross rails."

"Fantastic!" said Stevie.

"This calls for a celebration," Lisa said. "TD's, on me."

"Great!" Stevie said, quickly returning her saddle to its rack. "You know we're always happy to celebrate—and this is a terrific reason." TD's was a fantastic ice cream parlor not far from Pine Hollow. The Saddle Club went there often.

Lisa put her saddle back, too, and gathered up the saddle soap and sponges. "Let's ask the Pony Tails, too. I can't help but think that Amelia would like them, if she just gave them a chance."

"She might be ready to do that now," Carole said. "It was a pretty good riding lesson."

"If you're paying," Stevie said to Lisa, "you can invite the whole stable."

Lisa laughed. "Let's not go too far."

THE PONY TAILS were more than happy to eat ice cream instead of the bag lunches they'd brought with them. It wasn't long before all seven girls were crowded into TD's largest booth, happily consuming turtle sundaes, which were the special of the day. Even Stevie had ordered one—although she'd asked that strawberry sauce and crème de menthe be added to the caramel and hot fudge.

"That's disgusting," Amelia said, staring as Stevie lifted the first brown, pink, and green spoonful to her lips.

"Just don't watch her eat it," Lisa advised. Stevie always ate the strangest sundae combinations.

Carole took a big bite of ice cream and closed her eyes. When she opened them, she smiled at her friends. "Okay," she said, as if telling herself that she would be okay.

Lisa looked at Carole. Suddenly she could see how on edge Carole was. Not about the riding lesson, or Amelia. Starlight. It had to be. Lisa's heart sank. What had Carole learned?

Amelia dug into her sundae. "Isn't it funny," she said, "that this morning I didn't even want to ride Delilah?"

"Yeah, but why not?" Corey demanded. "Delilah's really sweet."

Amelia traced the outline of her place mat with her fingertip. "I wanted to ride Prancer," she explained.

"But that's silly," May interjected. "Prancer's too big for you—and she's really strong. She'd buck you off and throw you twice as far as Delilah did."

"I wouldn't ride Prancer for a hundred million dollars," Jasmine added.

"You would never have gotten to jump on Prancer," Corey said.

"Lisa rides Prancer," Stevie said softly.

"But Amelia's not Lisa," Corey argued.

"That's exactly right," said Lisa.

"I know," Amelia said. "I guess I know that now. But see, my mom and dad are always talking about Lisa. Like she's perfect or something. So." Amelia looked up, and the Pony Tails nodded as if they understood. Lisa understood, too. How hard it must have been for Amelia to have her parents bragging about Lisa, and then to have Lisa be so unfriendly. Lisa felt ashamed of her behavior. At least it all seemed to be working out now.

Amelia stirred her melting sundae until it was a thick brown puddle of goop. "Thanks for not laughing when I fell off," she said. "I bet it's been a long time since any of you fell off a horse."

Stevie and May burst out laughing before they could help themselves. After a moment Lisa, Carole, Corey, and Jasmine all joined in. "Like, we've all fallen off, like, half a hundred times," May said, through her giggles. "My last time was Friday."

"Remember the time Jasmine fell off right in that big patch of mud?" Corey said. She laughed so hard she had to cover her mouth.

"Or what about the time Carole landed in the creek?" Stevie hooted.

"Really," Carole said, "Starlight was very young then. And we won't even discuss Belle's little incident with the hay baler."

"Stevie rode her around the corner of the stable," Lisa

110

said, wiping tears of laughter from her eyes, "and she was bareback, and Belle saw this big, fearsome hay baler—"

"—a really scary, monstrous machine—" Carole added with relish.

"—smaller than your average tractor, and turned off, for Pete's sake, it wasn't making any noise or anything. I could have killed that mare—" Stevie sputtered.

"Belle whirled so fast that Stevie was hanging on by one leg and a handful of mane, and then Belle ran back into the stable and slammed to a stop—" Lisa laughed so hard she couldn't continue.

"—and I slammed to the ground, and landed right at Max's feet," Stevie concluded. "It was a little embarrassing. But I bet Lisa never told you about her first ride at Pine Hollow—her first ride ever."

"Did she fall off?" Amelia asked in amazement.

"No, I stayed on—barely," Lisa told her.

"Lisa was riding Patch in the indoor arena," Carole said. "And Veronica diAngelo slammed a door inside the stable, really loudly, and Patch spooked and took off running inside the arena. Poor Lisa didn't know what to do at all."

"It felt like half an hour before that horse stopped," Lisa remembered. "Part of me was scared to death, and part of me thought, *Wow! This is fun!*"

Amelia sucked on the end of her spoon. She seemed to be thinking about Lisa's story. Then her face lit up.

111

"I know exactly what you mean," she said excitedly, leaning forward. "A couple of weeks ago my instructor, Ruth, took our class out to the field that's across the street from our stable. It's across a really busy road, but the field's fenced, so it's safe. I ride after school, and by the end of the lesson it's always getting dark this time of year, and I guess the horses started thinking about their dinner, because when Ruthie told us to canter, all the horses took off for home!

"The worst part was, Ruth forgot to close the gate! So they were all galloping right for the road. Ruth started screaming, 'Sit up! Get them back! Turn them! Sit up!' "

Amelia yelled so loudly that several of the people in the restaurant turned around and looked at her. She paused to eat a spoonful of her sundae goop.

"What happened?" Corey asked.

Amelia grinned. "At first I thought, *I'm being run away with, I'm going to fall off, I'm going to die*. But then I realized that I wasn't falling off—my heels were down, like they were supposed to be, and, I felt pretty balanced. And then for a second it was really fun to be going that fast. And then I saw the road with all the cars on it just ahead, and I thought, *No, I am going to die*." She slurped another spoonful of sundae.

"Then what?" May asked impatiently.

"Well," said Amelia, "I thought, *I don't really want to die*,

112

so I sat back, pulled on the reins, and told Star she had to turn in a circle. And she really is a nice horse, even if she did try to run back for her dinner, and she slowed down and turned. I was in front of the rest of the class, and when Star stopped the other horses stopped, too. Nobody got hurt and nobody fell off. But one of the other girls was crying. I didn't feel like crying. I thought, *When I get good, I'll ride that fast on purpose—only not toward a highway!*"

Everyone at the table laughed. Lisa looked at Amelia's excited, transformed face. Despite her brattiness, there was suddenly something likable about her.

Apparently the Pony Tails thought so, too. "That's a great story," May said contentedly. "I like to ride fast, too. Maybe some day this week you could come over to my house and see the horses my dad is training. He's got a gelding that just came off the racetrack. It's wild." May took a sip of water and gave Amelia a saucy grin. "You can't ride him, though, so don't ask."

Amelia turned a little pink. "I'd like to see him," she said. "That sounds fun." She took a deep breath and added, "I'm sorry I made fun of your jodhpurs, May."

"That's okay," May said cheerfully. "When you've been riding long enough, yours will look just as disgusting."

Lisa could tell Amelia had never thought of it like that. She couldn't believe the change this one conversation had seemed to make in her cousin. Amelia was acting like a member of the human race. *Maybe she just needed a little help making friends*, Lisa thought.

"And I'm sorry I said Sam was funny-looking, Corey," Amelia added in a rush. "He's really cute. I wish I had a pony just as cute."

Corey grinned, then asked Lisa what time it was. "Gosh," she said when Lisa told her, "we've got to be back at Pine Hollow in half an hour, and there's this great new pony training book at the bookstore. I wanted to go look at it while we're here."

"Let's go!" Jasmine said, pushing back her chair. "C'mon, Amelia!" The younger girls all jumped up and clattered out the door.

The Saddle Club looked at the four empty chairs and four empty sundae dishes. "Here's your check," the waitress said cheerfully, slapping it on the table.

"I think we just got stiffed by the Pony Tails," Stevie said with a groan. "And I've only got three dollars. Carole?"

Lisa slapped a twenty-dollar bill on top of the check. "You can't have forgotten that this is my treat," she said. "Or, more precisely, my mother's treat. My mom gave me that this morning in case Amelia or I needed anything today."

"I think a celebration sundae was definitely necessary," Stevie said.

"I'm sure Amelia will still be a brat," Lisa said.

"But now she's a jumping brat," Stevie said.

114

"Carole," Lisa said softly, "I can tell something's wrong. What happened?"

Carole covered her face with her hands. After a long moment she steadied herself, dropped her hands, and set them firmly on the table. She looked at Lisa and Stevie. "I don't know anything yet," she said. "But I think it must be awful. Judy left me a note to call her, and she didn't say what was wrong."

"That doesn't mean it's bad," Stevie argued. "She just might have been in a hurry and didn't want to take the time to write."

"Maybe she needs to give you instructions on how to take care of him," Lisa suggested, "and it was too complicated to write down."

"Or maybe she just wants to break the bad news to me in person," Carole said. "I'm so afraid that Starlight will never be right again."

"You shouldn't worry about that until you know for sure," Lisa said.

"Remember," Stevie urged. "His hoof was hot. That *must* mean it's an abscess."

Carole took a deep breath. "When my mother got cancer," she said, "they did some tests first. Then when they got the results back, her doctor wouldn't tell her over the phone. He made her come into his office, so he could tell her in person."

"Right," Stevie said. "But Judy *is* going to tell you over the phone, so it can't be bad news. It's not the same."

"It's a lot the same," Carole said. "He could be permanently lame, Stevie. He really could be. I've thought so all weekend."

The waitress brought their change to the table. Lisa picked a quarter out of it. "Carole, I won't argue with you because you're right. It could be bad news. The only way we're going to find out is to call her, right now."

They went to the phone booth outside TD's and all crowded in. "She was gone when I called before," Carole said.

"If she's not in now, we'll walk back to Pine Hollow and try again," Lisa said firmly. Carole nodded. She dialed Judy's office.

"Hello? Oh, Judy, it's Carole." Stevie held up two fingers, crossed for good luck. Lisa held her breath. "He does? He is? Oh, wonderful!" She cupped the phone against her shoulder. "He's got an abscess! He'll be fine in a week!"

12

"LISA!" THERE WAS a pounding on the bedroom door. "Lisa, are you up yet?"

Lisa rolled over, pushed the covers off her face, and blinked sleepily at her bedside alarm clock. "No!" she said. "It's too early!"

"Lisa, you have to be awake if you're talking! We have to hurry! Can I come in?"

"Okay," Lisa muttered. She sat up just as Amelia rushed into the room. "Oh, geez," Lisa groaned. "You're already dressed. It's only seven o'clock, and Horse Wise doesn't start until nine. And we can't ride until after that, I already told you."

"I know." Amelia bounced on the corner of Lisa's bed. "I just couldn't sleep. Can't you get up yet?"

"And you're getting my bedspread dirty."

Amelia looked down at her grimy jodhpurs. She'd quit asking Mrs. Atwood to wash them. "Oops. Sorry." She bounced herself off the bed and plunked down on the floor. "Can I look at *Black Beauty* again? Are you going to get up?"

"Only if you are completely silent until I'm all the way dressed," Lisa said fiercely.

"Okay." Amelia rolled over and fished *Black Beauty* off the bottom shelf of Lisa's bookcase. Lisa sighed. She was used to quieter mornings, and she'd had an entire week of disruption. Still, after its awful start, the week of Amelia hadn't gone too badly. On Tuesday, still uncomfortable sleeping in the guest room, she'd informed Amelia that she wanted her own bedroom back. Amelia had thrown a pout, and in the end Lisa had loaned her one of her model horses to make up for it, but at least she'd slept comfortably from then on.

On Wednesday Amelia had had a bad lesson, and when she got done, she took off her helmet and threw it on the ground. Then, under Max's cold stare, she blushed, apologized, and retrieved it meekly. She also spent half an hour rerolling leg wraps to make up for it.

On Thursday Amelia stumbled in the aisle and ripped a

hole in her hundred-dollar jodhpurs. Lisa thought she seemed rather proud of it.

On Friday, which was yesterday, Max told her that she could go on a trail ride with The Saddle Club after Horse Wise's unmounted meeting. It was Amelia's first-ever trail ride. *No wonder she's so excited*, Lisa thought with a smile. Trail rides were wonderful.

Best of all, Judy had come back and opened the small abscess in Starlight's hoof. She hadn't had the proper instrument with her on her earlier visit. Carole had been diligent about wrapping and soaking it, and it was healing quickly.

"Lisa, are you dressed?" Amelia asked now.

"No," Lisa said. She was having trouble finding a clean pair of socks. Unthinkingly she grabbed one of the drawer handles that she'd been careful not to touch all week. Ink and grease smeared across her palm. She grabbed a tissue and tried to scrub it off.

"Because I just got to the part where Beauty falls down on the cobblestones—"

"Let me see your hands," Lisa interrupted. Amelia displayed two clean palms. Lisa sighed.

"Gosh, what happened?" Amelia asked. "Your fingers are purple!"

"Never mind."

"Well, anyway, when Beauty falls down—"

Lisa went to the bathroom to wash her hands. In just a little more than twenty-four hours, Amelia would be gone, and she would have peace and quiet again. Lisa had never realized how much she liked peace and quiet.

"Lisa?" Amelia poked her head in the bathroom door. "Aren't you dressed yet?"

AT BREAKFAST AMELIA hopped up and down so many times that Lisa didn't see how she could eat. "It's a long time until lunch," Lisa warned her.

"Not really," Amelia said. She leaned over and checked her reflection in the glass door of the oven. "Does my hair look okay?"

"Delilah will think you're beautiful," Lisa said dryly. To her surprise, her mother laughed. "She'll say," Lisa continued, " 'Who is this gorgeous girl? Why, it must be Amelia!' "

"My parents aren't going to recognize me when they see how well I ride," Amelia said. She sat down, grabbed a bite of toast, swung her legs, and jumped up again.

"Sit down," Mr. Atwood barked.

"I'm just going—"

"Sit *down*."

Amelia sat. "Because my mom and dad will be here by noon," she said. "Do you think we'll be back from our ride by then? I want to take a really long ride. Don't forget,

120

Uncle Richard, you promised to bring them straight to Pine Hollow."

"I won't even let them set foot in the house," Lisa's father promised solemnly. "As soon as they're out of their car, I'll put them in mine, and we'll rush straight to that stable." Lisa smothered a giggle.

"Good," Amelia said. "Because I know they're going to be really surprised. Don't you think they're going to be surprised, Lisa?"

Lisa smiled. "I sure do." At Amelia's request, she hadn't told her parents that Amelia had started jumping. Amelia wanted to keep it a secret until her own parents arrived.

Amelia's parents had flown back to New Jersey the night before. They'd arranged to drive down to Willow Creek, spend the night with the Atwoods, and start back home early Sunday morning. Lisa was looking forward to seeing her aunt and uncle, not least because they were taking Amelia away. She'd gotten to like a lot of things about her cousin, but Amelia was still very used to getting her own way, and Lisa realized that she was very used to her usual schedule. It would be a relief to hang around Pine Hollow without having to worry about Amelia.

WHEN MRS. ATWOOD let the girls out at Pine Hollow, Amelia ran toward the stable almost before the car had

121

stopped. Just as quickly, Carole came running out and swooped Lisa into a hug as she got out of the car. "Judy just left, and guess what!" she cried. "Starlight's fine! I can ride him again!"

"Wonderful!"

"Starlight's okay?" Amelia stuck her head back out the stable door and came flying back to Carole. "Is he really okay?"

Carole's eyes shined with happiness. "He really is. So I can go on your trail ride with you."

"Yeah! I'll go tell Delilah!" Amelia scampered back to the building.

"No running in the stable!" Carole shouted after her.

"Sorry!" Amelia called back.

"I've told her that three hundred times," Lisa said. "She doesn't listen."

"She listens," Carole said. "She just doesn't remember."

"And yet somehow," Lisa countered, "she had been able to remember every single little thing Max or you have taught her all week, from how to wrap a horse's leg to the difference between Pelham and Kimblewicke bits, not to mention the entire plot of Black Beauty, which I believe she's now reading for the third straight time."

"That's because she wants to run, whether she's in the stable or not," Carole said.

Lisa rolled her eyes in agreement. "I'm so happy about Starlight, Carole. I hoped and hoped he'd be better by today."

"Because you don't want to go on a trail ride without Max's esteemed assistant instructor along to handle Amelia," Carole teased.

"Because it hasn't seemed right riding without *both* of my best friends," Lisa countered.

"HI, MAY!" AMELIA said as they went into the office for the Horse Wise meeting.

"Hi!" May shouted. She scooted over a little to make room for Amelia to sit. A lot of the other kids who had been in mini-camp with Amelia smiled and talked to her, too. She had made some friends.

"I saw that your ponies are still here," Amelia said to the Pony Tails. "I thought Mr. Grover was coming to get them last night."

"He had to go see a horse for a client instead," May explained. "And this morning he's taking one of his young horses to a one-day dressage show, just for experience. He's going to pick our ponies up when he gets back this evening."

"Great!" Amelia said. "That means you can come on our trail ride!"

123

"Super!" Jasmine said.

"Oh no," Lisa groaned. "I thought we'd just have to keep an eye on Amelia. Now there's four of them."

"The Pony Tails are pretty self-sufficient," Stevie reminded her.

"As long as they don't start wanting to gallop," Lisa said. "They'll get Amelia all fired up."

"Starlight won't be galloping," Carole said. "Just walking and trotting. That will be enough for Amelia, too, and it ought to be enough for the Pony Tails."

"It'll have to be," Lisa said resolutely.

IT WAS. AFTERWARD, even Lisa had to admit that she'd rarely been on such a nice trail ride. The weather was perfect for winter—crystal clear, with a warm sun and no wind—and the ground was firm. Amelia was so euphoric by the idea of riding outside a ring, in actual woods, that she listened to everything the older girls said, and Delilah pricked her ears and stepped out with obvious enjoyment. The Pony Tails seemed to feel some responsibility toward Amelia, too.

"Make sure you never get too relaxed," Corey advised her. "You don't want to be tense, either, but remember that anything can happen out on a trail. A deer might suddenly leap across the path and startle your horse, so you've always got to be ready for something to happen."

Amelia sat up a little straighter. "Oh, look at that stream!" she exclaimed.

They looked. It was the same stream they passed or crossed on every single trail ride they ever went on.

"That's Willow Creek. In warm weather we take off our boots and go wading in it," Lisa said.

"It's so beautiful!" Amelia said.

Carole looked down at the creek. She liked it, but she saw it so often that she rarely looked at it closely. Amelia was right—it flowed eagerly over rocks, through curving banks that in summer were overhung with ferns. Today, back on Starlight again, Carole felt as joyful as Amelia. "It is beautiful," she said fervently.

Amelia turned in the saddle. "You are so lucky," she said to Lisa. "At my stable, we don't have any trails at all."

Lisa knew she was lucky. "If you keep taking lessons," she said, "next time when you come, we can go on a really long ride and jump some logs and everything."

Amelia beamed. Stevie rode close to Lisa. " 'Next time when you come'?" she repeated. "Did I hear that correctly? I couldn't have!"

Lisa shrugged. "Next time, I'll make sure she doesn't come for a whole week," she said.

When they rode back out of the woods, into an open field next to Pine Hollow, they could see the Atwoods' station wagon waiting in the drive.

"Oh!" Amelia yelled. "Mom! Dad!" She stood in the stirrups and waved, but the people standing outside the car didn't seem to notice. Amelia dropped back into the saddle and clucked to Delilah.

"Amelia—" Lisa warned.

Amelia made a face. "I *know*. No trotting back to the stable. But we can walk fast, can't we?"

"Mom!" When they reached the driveway, Amelia bent down to hug and kiss her mother and father.

"Wow," Amelia's father, Mr. Brandon, said. "That's a big horse."

"This is Delilah," Amelia said importantly. "She's a very good horse. Not quite as nice as Star, of course."

"Well," Mr. Brandon said, a touch uncertainly, "she certainly looks like something. She's very big."

"You can pat her, Dad, she likes that," Amelia told him.

"Um-hm," he said, but he didn't move to touch the horse. Delilah turned her head to sniff him, and he jumped. Lisa grinned. Her uncle William didn't seem too comfortable around horses. She wondered if he'd ever seen Amelia ride before.

"Is she a Thoroughbred?" Lisa's aunt inquired.

"Yes," Carole said firmly. "She's thoroughly well bred." Lisa, Stevie, and the Pony Tails all giggled, and even Amelia looked amused. Delilah was not a Thoroughbred or any type

126

of purebred, but Lisa liked Carole's way of answering the question.

"Climb down from that horse and show us around," Mr. Brandon offered. "I hear you had a pretty nice week."

Amelia looked at Carole. "First I have something really neat to show you," she said. "Right, Carole?"

"Right," Carole said. She dismounted crisply while Lisa and Stevie grinned. "Just let me run Starlight inside."

"Carole's been teaching me all week," Amelia explained. "She and Max and Red taught the camp."

"That's nice," Mrs. Brandon said. "It won't take too long, will it? We're eager to get you back to your aunt's house so you can tell us everything about your week."

Lisa sighed. Everything that was important to Amelia's week had happened right here.

"Aren't you guys going to take your ponies in?" Stevie asked Jasmine.

"No way," Jasmine said. "We're watching this."

Lisa and Stevie looked at each other and grinned again.

"Is it some sort of secret?" Mr. Brandon asked.

Amelia overheard and turned to him with a smile. "This is a big, big secret," she said. "You're going to be very impressed."

Carole walked out of the stable and over to the fenced riding ring. She opened the gate, and Amelia rode Delilah

127

inside. While Amelia trotted Delilah around the edge of the ring, Carole carefully set up a row of four tiny gymnastic fences, one right after the other.

"Okay," Carole said to Amelia. The younger girl steadied Delilah's trot, then carefully guided her toward the row of cross rails. Just before the first fence, she rose slightly in the saddle and grabbed a handful of Delilah's mane. Delilah jumped the fences tidily, one after another. Amelia stayed rock steady in the saddle.

"Yay!" Stevie and Lisa and the Pony Tails cheered.

"She's really getting good," Stevie said.

"She's been working very hard," Lisa replied. "Of course, talent runs in the family!"

Amelia trotted to the end of the ring, turned Delilah, and trotted quickly back to her parents, a rapturous smile on her face. "What do you think?" she asked. "Weren't we good? Wasn't Delilah amazing?"

"Very nice," Mrs. Brandon said with a big smile. "That was awfully nice, dear. You looked just like one of the pictures in *Town & Country* magazine."

Lisa and Stevie looked at each other. Amelia's parents didn't understand what an accomplishment it was for her to be jumping already. They didn't look impressed at all. "Well," Lisa whispered, "my aunt is like my mother, so you can't really expect her to be horse-crazy."

"No," Stevie said, "but your mother's all right."

"So is my aunt, mostly," Lisa said. She watched Amelia dismount, loosen Delilah's girth, and run the stirrups up before hugging her parents. "But I think there are a lot of things about Amelia that she doesn't understand."

Stevie nodded. "Poor Amelia."

"I never thought I'd say this," Lisa said, "but I agree."

"I CAN'T BELIEVE it's raining," Carole said. She stared out the window of TD's. The sky was overcast, and sheets of rain fell steadily from the dark gray clouds. It was a miserable day.

"At least we're inside, where it's warm," Lisa said.

"At least we're eating hot fudge sundaes," Stevie added. "It was nice of your mom to bring us here, Lisa, and it was even nicer of her to treat us. That's twice this week."

"We earned it," Lisa said, in a voice of satisfaction. "My mom even said so. She said she was grateful that I'd taken up my vacation time with Amelia. Until she said that, I wasn't even sure she realized I was doing it." Lisa checked her watch. "Amelia should be almost back to New Jersey by now."

"Phew," Stevie said. "I mean, the week turned out okay, but I'm still glad it's over."

"You can say that again," Lisa agreed.

"Three times over," said Carole.

"Phew," Stevie said. "I mean, the week—"

"I was just kidding," Carole interrupted quickly. Stevie grinned, and Carole flipped a tiny blob of hot fudge off her spoon toward Stevie.

"No throwing food," their usual waitress barked as she passed their table. Carole hid her spoon under the table. Stevie made a face, and the waitress laughed and walked away.

"I wonder what she thinks is so funny," Stevie said grumpily. Carole and Lisa laughed.

"She's probably relieved to see you eating something normal for once," Carole joked.

Stevie looked disgusted. "I can't believe you made me order a regular hot fudge sundae. My reputation will be ruined!"

Lisa shrugged airily. "My mother specifically said that she'd buy us all hot fudge sundaes. Besides, Stevie, eating normal food once in a while won't kill you. Have pity on Carole and me."

"Okay," Stevie said. "Since you had your cousin all week, and Carole had to nurse Starlight, I guess I can eat a plain sundae. It seems like an equivalent sacrifice."

Carole rolled her eyes. "Lisa, aren't we lucky to have such a good friend?"

Lisa set her spoon down. "Yes," she said seriously. "I'm lucky to have both of you. I don't know what I would have done without you this week. Amelia would have driven me right up a tree."

"I'm lucky, too," Carole said softly. "You're right. Thank you."

"Me too," Stevie added. "I don't get next week's allowance until Wednesday, and I'm flat broke, so if it weren't for you, Lisa, I wouldn't be eating any kind of ice cream at all." She said it in her most sincere voice, and Lisa threw a wadded-up napkin at her. Stevie ducked. The napkin hit the waitress, who calmly picked it up, put it back on the table, smiled at them all, and walked away.

"This goofy mood of hers is giving me the creeps," Stevie said. Carole snorted.

"Did you notice how much better Amelia got once she realized she was going to have to do as she was told?" Lisa asked. "I mean, she didn't turn into an angel or anything, but she was a lot better. I could at least stand to be around her."

"Well, sure," Carole said. "Raising kids is probably a lot

like training horses. You can't let horses get away with doing whatever they want, either."

"Trust Carole to compare Amelia to a horse," Stevie said to Lisa.

"I'm serious," Carole said with a grin. "Think about it. She never really got punished, she just wasn't allowed to get away with things, and she came around just like a horse. I'd say we got her green-broke this week. And even if she did start out monstrously, she didn't do anyone any permanent harm."

Stevie snorted. "Except the hobbyhorse."

Carole's face fell. "Oh. That's right."

"Actually," Lisa said, "my parents took the hobbyhorse to be restored. They said the work will take a while, but in the end the hobbyhorse should look almost as good as new."

"Almost," Stevie said glumly.

"Yeah," Lisa admitted. "You'll still be able to tell that it was broken. But really, it was the most amazing thing, I've been dying to tell you guys. You know how my parents didn't say a single word about the hobbyhorse all week?"

Carole and Stevie nodded.

"Well," Lisa said, "last night at dinner my mom asked my aunt and uncle if they remembered seeing the horse, and they said of course. Then my mom looked straight at Amelia and said, 'It seems there was a little accident this week.' "

133

"You're kidding!" Stevie said. "You told us your parents thought it was your fault."

"That's what I thought!" Lisa said. "Best of all, Amelia told her parents that it was mostly her fault. She said it was an accident, and she didn't mean to break it, but she pretty much admitted that it was her fault. I said it was a little bit my fault, too—because it was."

"Amazing," Stevie declared. "I never thought she'd actually say she did something wrong."

"So right away my uncle said he would pay for the hobbyhorse's restoration," Lisa continued. "And Amelia said she had twenty bucks saved from her Christmas money, and she'd give that. My dad accepted it, too. I mean, I know restoring the horse is going to cost a lot more than twenty dollars, but at least Amelia's trying."

Carole's face took on a maternal glow. "One of my very first students," she said happily.

"The best part is realizing that my parents believed my side of the story all along," Lisa said. "I always thought they were siding with Amelia, but this morning Mom said they just didn't want to start a major fight with her. Mom said she was proud of all I did for Amelia this week. She said it was a big responsibility." Lisa smiled. She couldn't really express how happy she was that her parents had known about Amelia and the hobbyhorse, but she had a feeling her friends understood.

"I couldn't believe how much responsibility it took to be an assistant instructor," Carole said, after a pause. "I mean, we work around the stables all the time, right? But taking care of those kids was totally different." She leaned forward. "Have you ever seen anyone put a saddle on a horse backwards?" she asked. "Little Wendy Casto did it twice. The first time she went ahead and mounted, even though I'd told her not to."

"She sat in the saddle backwards?" Lisa asked. "Wouldn't that be uncomfortable?"

"Oh no," Carole said, with a grin. "She got into the saddle correctly—only she didn't understand why she was facing the horse's tail!"

Stevie and Lisa laughed uproariously. "Taking care of Starlight was a pretty big responsibility this week, too," Lisa added. "Don't think Stevie and I didn't realize how many hours you spent soaking and bandaging Starlight's hoof. And I know Judy said your care was part of the reason he healed so quickly."

Carole blushed. "Taking care of Starlight never feels like work, no matter how much time I spend doing it. I love him so much."

Stevie smiled. "Well, I didn't have as hard of a week as either of you, but I'm still pretty tired." She yawned. *It's a good thing it rained today*, she thought. She would hardly have had the energy to ride Belle anyway.

135

"And tomorrow we've got to go back to school," Lisa said. She slumped against the tabletop. She could barely move. She wondered when she'd ever have the urge to ride again.

Carole looked out the window at the cold, steady rain. What sounded best to her right now was an afternoon spent curled beneath her afghan with her cat, Snowball, and a stack of the latest horse magazines. "You know," she said slowly, "it's supposed to stop raining tonight. If we're lucky, we can go on a trail ride tomorrow after school."

Stevie and Lisa sat up straight. "Oh, good!" they said in a single breath.

ABOUT THE AUTHOR

BONNIE BRYANT is the author of many books for young readers, including novelizations of movie hits such as *Teenage Mutant Ninja Turtles* and *Honey, I Blew Up the Kid*, written under her married name, B. B. Hiller.

Ms. Bryant began writing The Saddle Club in 1986. Although she had done some riding before that, she intensified her studies then and found herself learning right along with her characters Stevie, Carole, and Lisa. She claims that they are all much better riders than she is.

Ms. Bryant was born and raised in New York City. She still lives there, in Greenwich Village, with her two sons.